BAD MOON ARISING

Outcasts, Book One

CL Mustafic

A NineStar Press Publication

Published by NineStar Press
P.O. Box 91792,
Albuquerque, New Mexico, 87199 USA.
www.ninestarpress.com

Bad Moon Arising

Printed in the USA
First Edition
July, 2018

Print ISBN: 978-1-949340-06-8

Also available in eBook, ISBN: 978-1-949340-05-1

Warning: This book contains sexually explicit content, which may only be suitable for mature readers.

In a sleepy trailer park in the backwoods of Minnesota lake country, there lies a secret—threatened by a Grindr hookup gone bad.

Clay Anderson gets more than he bargained for when, in a moment of passion, he bites his Grindr hookup hard enough to draw blood. The man's reaction isn't as reassuring as Clay hoped, but of all the consequences Clay considered, lycanthropy wasn't among them.

Damian Maccon leads a simple life as part of the Outcast pack. Not realizing at first that Clay swallowed his blood during their wild romp, he feels responsible when it's evident that Clay has become infected. Worse, he now has a new werewolf on his hands until Clay learns the rules, and he has to oversee Clay's decision to choose a mate within the pack.

Damian thinks his biggest problem is that Clay hates him, but when Clay chooses Damian's abusive ex-boyfriend, Blaine, he goes on full alert. Can he save Clay from the same fate that befell him at Blaine's hands?

To Christina Quinn, you dared me and now you have to take responsibility for the havoc you created.

Chapter One

CLAY

Sitting in the back booth of the Blue Moon Bar and Grill—the only openly gay-friendly spot in the small city I worked in—I ran my finger over the screen of my phone, trying to gather up enough courage to tap the picture I'd been staring at for the past ten minutes. Touching the pic brought up his profile, which I'd already memorized. The green light told me he was online and only a few miles away from my current location. I liked his pic. It wasn't very often Grindr users in my rural area posted pictures of their faces. Previous experience had taught me most of the app's users were closeted and/or straight guys who liked to suck the occasional cock and worried their dude bros would download the app as a joke and see them there. But this guy had no such issue, and boy, was I glad.

Of course, on the heels of that thought came another: it probably wasn't a real pic of the guy. As I stared into the mismatched eyes—one a light green, the other a pale blue—I had a feeling he was catfishing, but there was only one way to find out for sure. Tapping the picture of the shaggy, sandy-blond-haired, scruffy-faced man brought up the chat, but I hesitated a moment. His user name was MoonGazer, which made me think of a nerdy guy with a telescope. Suddenly I had a vision of the guy sitting in his room spying on the hot guy next door, which gave me the boost of confidence I needed to send a message.

[hey]

I sent the one word and immediately wanted to take it back. I should have said something like *Hey, sexy, want to hook up?* but that wasn't me, and I couldn't change the person I was, even on Grindr. Half a beer later, he responded.

[hey urself]

My palms were sweaty as I stared at the words and tried to formulate a response, but he beat me to it.

[r u l%kin 2 h%k up]

All the moisture left my mouth, so I picked up my beer and chugged the rest before I sent another one-word message.

[yep]

[whr u at]

Shit, he moved fast, but this is what I wanted, and he must have liked my pic enough to give it a go. My profile pic was only my chest. Yeah, I know it's a cliché, but I had a great body, whereas my face? Well, my face wasn't my best feature.

[you know where the blue moon is]

[b thr in 10]

I almost dropped my phone, but instead, I juggled it and managed to avoid it hitting the table.

[I'm in the back booth, black hair, red shirt]

What the hell was I doing? Oh, fuck it. I needed to get laid, and even if the guy wasn't remotely as hot as his picture, I could turn him around and do it without having to look at him.

[gotcha]

Well, he wasn't going to be much for conversation; that was for sure. After ordering a shot of vodka and another beer for courage, I sat back in my booth, eyes glued to the front door as I sipped my beer to soothe the burn from the stronger alcohol. The minutes ticked by slowly, and then the door opened and all the air in the room was sucked out when he stepped into the bar.

He waved to the burly bartender before turning his head and surveying the room. It was like a god had appeared, and I wasn't the only one who noticed. Every set of eyes followed the tall, muscular man as he sauntered across the room. I wanted to shrink down into the booth. His picture hadn't done him justice, and I knew I was about to be rebuked in a horrible fashion when he saw what he'd come to meet.

The moment he spotted me will be forever etched into my mind. His mismatched eyes settled on my face, and a predatory grin spread across his lips. Droplets of sweat rolled down my back and pooled in the crack of my ass, making me shift at the uncomfortable sensation. His gaze never left me as he made his way to my booth before dropping down on the bench across from me.

"Hey there, black hair, red shirt," he said, in a slow, sexy, Southern-tinged drawl. His voice was low and gravely, and it stirred all sorts of feelings in me—well, in my pants at least.

"Hey." God, I sounded like the nerd I'd been hoping he'd turn out to be. He chuckled, and the hairs on my arms stood up.

"Want to get out of here?"

Straight to the point, like his messages; at least he wasn't at all about false advertising. Nodding, I grabbed my wallet and pulled out a twenty to leave on the table to cover my tab and tip. We stood at the same time, and he waited for me to put my jacket on before he headed for the door. We didn't say anything more as we left the bar. I followed him out into the parking lot, but then stopped when I realized I had no clue where we were going since my car was parked in the opposite direction from the one he was heading.

"Do you have someplace we can go?" I asked. I could take him back to my place, but that meant a twenty-minute drive, and I wasn't sure I wanted him to know where I lived. He could be a serial killer for all I knew.

"I got a camper on the back of my truck. That work for you?" His grin widened into a smile when he looked back over his shoulder at me and pointed to the brand-new four-door extended-box pickup that did indeed have one of those tacky campers attached to it. His wasn't too bad, since it was a newer model, but it was still something of an atrocity. I wondered briefly if he lived in there, but then decided I didn't care. It wasn't as if I was looking to marry the guy.

"I guess that will do." I shrugged and went to the small door at the back, but he'd gone to the driver's side door of the truck.

"I think we should at least drive out of the city a bit. Wouldn't want to scare the good folks when you start screaming my name," he said, with a wink, before opening his door and climbing in without even waiting to see if I'd follow.

I hesitated. Did I really want to get in the truck with this guy? My brain said it wasn't the best idea, but my cock didn't agree. I guess the small head won out because next thing I knew, I was sitting in the big leather seat next to him, and he was driving out of the city. There was no conversation. I didn't expect there to be an in-depth discussion on environmental politics or anything, but a bit of chitchat would have been nice while we drove for over ten minutes looking for a place to pull off that provided us some tree cover to hide the truck from the traffic on the highway.

He put the truck into park and shut off the engine before he turned to me. "You ready to do this?"

"Yeah, let's go." I opened my door and jumped down. The sound of his door opening made the situation feel real to me in a way it hadn't before. Something about the guy seemed off, and I wondered, if I were to start running, would he give chase or simply laugh at me? I made my feet move and met him at the back of the truck.

He unlocked and pulled the door of the camper open and then waited for me. There was no step on the outside of the camper, so I stood there trying to think of a way to climb up and into it without looking like a fool. The guy harrumphed as he let go of the door, grabbed my waist, and, lifting me like I was a ten-pound bag of potatoes, dumped me into the darkness of the camper.

"Geez, impatient, are we?" I grumbled when he followed me in, shut the door, and clicked on a light. I'd never been in a pickup camper before, so I was surprised when the light revealed a space that looked relatively comfortable even for a man the size of the guy who'd just shoved me through the door. It also looked lived-in.

"I ain't got all night, and you looked like you needed a little boost." His grin was back as he moved to the seating area and started converting it into a bed. I was having a hard time getting over that accent and the way he talked. He sounded every bit the redneck hick who resided in a camper, and I wasn't sure if that was a massive turn-on or not.

"Isn't there a bed in this thing?" I asked because I'm an idiot and I had nothing else to say.

"There is, but it's up in the loft and last time I tried fuckin' up there, I got a knob on the back of my head for my troubles. This works better." He went to a cabinet and pulled out a sheet that he threw haphazardly over the bed. He then kicked off his shoes, shrugged out of his jacket, pulled his shirt over his head, and started on his belt buckle. "You gonna get naked, or do you have some sorta magic that lets you fuck in your clothes?" he asked when I sat there staring at his tattooed torso.

"I...uh...no." I began to unbutton my shirt as he laughed at me.

Soon we were both standing there naked, his eyes sweeping over my body, and I swear he growled before he tackled me back onto the bed. He pinned me down, and just when I thought he was going to kiss me, he veered left and sniffed my neck—no, sniffed is not the word for what he did. He snuffled at my neck and I laughed because it tickled, and of course, the laugh made me snort, which is not the sexiest sound a guy can make.

"You smell like fear. Are you afraid of me?" he asked when he was done sampling my aroma.

"What? No. How can you smell fear? Are you part bloodhound?"

He chuckled, and then he did kiss me, hard. He was all tongue and teeth. I tried to keep up with him, but in the end, I let his mouth have its way with mine. It was fucking hot! I'd never had a guy who was so energetic about something like a kiss, and my cock was rigid against his hairy thigh. I rocked my hips, and he got the idea and shifted so that our groins matched up. He started humping me, and I knew if he wasn't careful, I'd come just from that and ruin any plans he'd had of doing something more.

I turned my head to free up my mouth to tell him so, but once my lips were no longer there for him to maul, he started in on my neck and all I could do was moan. I was on the brink when he nipped at my earlobe and said something I hadn't expected to hear.

"Want you to fuck me."

Paralyzed by the thought of this man wanting me to fuck him, I lay there like a moron. I had been expecting either mutual blowjobs or maybe for him to ask to fuck me, but never in my wildest dreams had I thought I'd be the one fucking him.

"Did you hear me?" he asked, pulling back to look down at me with those strange but alluring eyes. I nodded. "Is that not something you want to do?" His brow creased as he frowned, and I finally found my voice.

"No, I mean, no it's not something I don't want to do. I want to. Christ, I really want to!" Okay, that might have been a bit too enthusiastic, but it wiped the frown clean off his face.

"Good, I'll get the stuff." Getting up on his knees, he rummaged through one of the kitchen drawers that happened to be right next to the makeshift bed. He pulled out a handful of condoms and a huge tube of lube and dropped them on the bed next to me. "Hurry up and get one of 'em on."

Not needing to be told twice, I ripped into one of the condoms and rolled it down my hard shaft while he climbed over me to the center of the bed. Just looking at him there on all fours made my dick throb, and getting the lube applied without coming was a true test of my willpower. I did manage to hold back the groin geyser long enough to get in position behind him. Pressing my hands to his muscular cheeks, I spread him. I thought to tease his hole with my finger, maybe even get some lube up in there, but he jerked away.

"Just do it," he said. His head hung low between his shoulders as he pressed back, offering his ass up to me.

"Are you sure?"

"Fuck, man. Just fuck me already!"

I grabbed his hip with one hand and my cock in the other and did what he wanted. Sliding the head of my cock into the tight, hot heat of another man's ass was probably the hottest three seconds of any sexual encounter and I liked to savor the moment, since it was a rare occurrence for me, but the guy didn't let me enjoy it. He pushed back, and I watched, fascinated, as his ass quickly swallowed my full length.

"Fuck, give a guy some warning," I groaned, and that fucker chuckled at me again. I slapped his ass, and that got his attention. "You want me to fuck you, or are you the one in charge here?" I smacked his other cheek and had to admit the sound it made was very satisfying.

"What are you waiting for? Do it, hard."

Gripping his hips, I pulled out and slammed back in, making him grunt with the force of it.

"Fuck, finally."

His groaned words equal parts pissed me off and turned my crank, and that's all I needed to give it to him good. I lost all my earlier worries and let go, fucking him with an abandon I never would have tried with any other guy, but this guy had asked for it. His body shifted when he reached under himself to jerk his cock, and I had to readjust my stance, which must have been a good thing, because upon my next thrust, he howled. I looked around since the sound was such an uncanny imitation of a wolf I wondered if maybe one had wandered out of the woods and had somehow gotten into the camper.

My one moment of inattention earned me a growl because I'd stopped moving my hips. He pushed up off the bed so he ended up on his knees and sitting in my lap, burying my cock even farther up his ass. Using his thigh muscles, he bounced on my cock. I wrapped my arms around his chest and held on for the ride. Staring at the back of his sweaty neck put ideas in my head, and I bent forward to get a taste, but his shudder egged me into doing more than kissing the moist, overheated skin. I nibbled, and that produced a moan as he tilted his head to expose more of his neck for me. I took it as an invitation and bit down, making him howl again.

His ass clenched down on my cock as he came, shooting his come out over the sheet he'd laid down earlier. He only missed about two beats before moving again, and I was done. I don't know what possessed me to do it, but as I came, sheathed inside his quivering hole, I bit down harder on his neck and the coppery taste of blood filled my mouth.

"Ugh, fuck." He reached back and grabbed my hair, holding my head in place over the wound when I tried to pull away.

I couldn't stop the automatic reflex to swallow and cringed as his blood made its way down my throat, before he let me go and slumped forward. Remembering to hold the condom while my cock slid out of his ass, I sat there staring at him, wondering if I'd just swallowed a death sentence. What if he had some kind of disease or something, and now I had it too?

"Is there a bathroom in this thing?" I asked but was sure there couldn't possibly be one.

"Yeah, that door there. But don't flush the toilet unless you gotta shit," he mumbled without moving to indicate which door was "that door there."

I half expected him to be joking, having meant the outside door, but when I got off the bed, I saw what he was talking about, and once opened, found there to be a tiny sink and toilet. I dropped the condom in the small wastebasket and then turned on the water. Knowing it wasn't going to do me any good, I washed my mouth out with water. I looked at the door before sticking my finger in my mouth to try to gag myself. Maybe if I vomited up the blood, it would keep me from catching anything he had. I was desperate, but nothing doing. I couldn't make myself puke; damn blowjobs had done fuck-all to my gag reflex.

Banging on the door scared the crap out of me. "You okay in there? You didn't fall in, did ya?"

"No, I'm fine. I'm only washing my hands," I called back. I turned the sink off and looked for something to dry my hands on, but there was nothing but toilet paper. Taking a deep breath, I opened the door with one of my dripping hands and stepped out, ready to apologize for biting him so hard.

"I thought maybe you got lost in there." His grin was back and so were his underwear and T-shirt, which was a little bit disappointing.

"Yeah, it's pretty huge. I almost asked for breadcrumbs." My joke fell flat because I got another of those frowns from him. "I'm kidding." I went to the pile of clothes and started dressing, wanting to get out of there before I could make myself look like a bigger idiot.

He managed to get dressed faster than me and stood there waiting once again for a reverse of the earlier scene. I kept my head down because I was afraid if I made eye contact, I might have to talk to him. Once I was fully dressed and had zipped my jacket, he opened the door. I hustled to get out right away so he wouldn't feel the need to help me again.

He shut the door after dropping down and winked at me before turning to go to the front of the truck. I trudged to the passenger's side and got in. I still wanted to tell him I was sorry for the bite, but I didn't know how to bring it up. He wasn't much of a talker, so I couldn't casually mention it in the course of the conversation. I sat there, hands folded in my lap, and watched the nothingness of the dark night pass us by until we hit the city limits.

"My car is over there." I pointed to my beat-up blue Honda Civic, which had seen better days, as he pulled into the parking lot of the Blue Moon. He stopped right next to my car and turned to look at me, and once again I noticed how unsettling his bicolored eyes were. Even in the dim light from the dashboard and the parking lot lights, it was eerie. Like two different people were sharing the same head, and both were looking out at me in judgment.

"So, that was fun, thanks," he said.

"Ah, yeah, but before I go, I want to tell you something." I shifted in my seat, ready to say I was sorry, but he held up a hand to stop me.

"No names, I'm not looking for anything more than a quick hookup."

My mouth dropped open but then snapped closed. Of course, a guy who looked like him probably had guys wanting to do it again all the time, so I could respect that he was only looking to get off and nothing more. I nodded to indicate I got it, but I was still going to apologize whether he wanted to hear it or not. It was how my mom had raised me, and there was no going against that ingrained bullshit.

"It's not that. I wasn't going to tell you my name or ask if we could do it again." My statement didn't have as big an effect on him as his did on me, but he did quirk a brow as if he was surprised and maybe interested in what I had to say. "I just wanted to say I was sorry for biting you so hard. I didn't mean to break the skin and, yeah, I'm sorry."

"You broke the skin?" The cocky way he'd been holding himself all night—like he knew he was the shit—fell away, and a worried look turned to horrified when I nodded to confirm what he'd heard was true. "Shit, did you get blood in your mouth?"

Fuck! I knew it! He had something, and now I was going to die! "I did and I think I swallowed a little bit too. Please tell me you don't have anything that's going to kill me," I pleaded.

He shook his head. "Fuck, goddamn it." Slamming his hand down on the steering wheel, he made us both jump when he accidentally hit the horn.

I didn't take his reaction as a sign that I didn't have anything to worry about, and I was ready to go full-out panic mode when he reached over and grabbed my arm. I jerked away as if his touch could do more harm than swallowing his fucking blood already had.

"Hey, it's not that. I'm not sick. I don't have anything that's going to kill you. It's just not a good thing to be drinking other people's blood," he said. The words did nothing to calm my fears after his earlier reaction. "I swear to you that I don't have a disease that will kill you."

Well, that was reassuring, but what about the ones that wouldn't kill me? After taking a few deep breaths, I nodded. Freaking out would do me no good. The damage was already done, but that wasn't going to stop me from going to the clinic and asking the doctor if there was a way I could cut the risk of catching anything that could have possibly been in his blood. "Okay, I believe you. I have to go." I clutched the door handle, but once again he grabbed me.

"My name's Damian Maccon," he said. I turned to look at him, wondering why he was suddenly having a change of heart about the no-name-exchanging thing. It only made me suspicious about his claim of not having any diseases. "If I gave you a deadly disease, do you think I'd tell you my name?"

"I have no idea, and I guess I don't care. What's done is done. It was my fault anyway. I really have to go now. Thanks for the...sex." Not letting him stop me again, I got out and was locked in my car in record time. He didn't leave, which made me nervous enough to not head home right away when I pulled out of the parking lot, instead driving to the all-night grocery store. Only after I parked, looked around, and found no sign of his truck did I put the car back into gear and drive home.

Chapter Two

DAMIAN

After parking my truck in front of the doublewide trailer on the edge of the compound, I shut off the engine and let my head fall forward until my forehead was resting on the wheel. I wasn't happy about having to go in and tell Pete and Willard about what had happened. It wasn't about the sex. If it was about that, they would only slap me on the back and ask if it was good. No, it was about the bite and the blood. Shit, he'd swallowed my blood. I sat up and punched the steering wheel with the flat of my hand, accidentally hitting the horn for the second time that night and sending a sharp bleat out into the night. When the front porch light came on, I knew it was time to get out and face the music.

Willard met me at the door after what felt like the longest damn walk of my life, and I've taken some walks of shame in my time. His brow furrowed when he saw my face, and he asked, "Whiskey or tea?"

"Whiskey."

He nodded. "All right, come on in. I'll get Pete." He let me pass before he shut the door, then snapped off the porch light.

I took a seat on the sofa and adopted the posture of the truly repentant, even before I confessed my blunder. Hearing Willard tell Pete I was there waiting for them and had chosen whiskey instead of tea, I knew I only had moments left as part of the Outcast pack. There was no way they wouldn't exile me for this fuckup.

A liter bottle of Jack was plonked down on the table in front of me, and then three glasses joined it. Pete sat on the couch next to me, and Willard took to his recliner right across from us. I waited until Pete had poured a healthy three fingers of the amber liquid into three glasses and they each took theirs from the table. Grabbing mine with an unsteady hand, I sat back on the couch and took a deep breath before throwing the whiskey back. I let the burn in the pit of my stomach center me.

"I might have a problem." *Understatement of the year goes to...*

"Tell us what happened and let us decide if you do or not," Willard said. It was what I'd expected him to say because it was his standard line.

One time I'd killed a farmer's cow and thought it was the end of the world. Pete and Willard had taken care of the situation after I'd told them, so therefore it hadn't been a problem, which was why he always said it was up to them to decide if it was one or not. I wished this time it was something as simple as dead livestock.

"I was with someone tonight, and he might have—no, he did, swallow some of my blood." There. I'd said it. Now, all I could do was wait for the damnation to be dealt out.

"You're sure?" Pete put his hand on my thigh. I'm sure he thought it was a comforting gesture, but to me it felt like he was pinning me down with that one slender hand.

"He said he did. I can't be sure because I didn't even realize he'd broken the skin, and it had healed by the time I'd gotten a look at it."

"If you're not one hundred percent certain—"

"And lycanthropy isn't easy to spread. He'd have had to swallow a good amount, and there's still a chance he might not catch it," Willard interrupted Pete.

"But there's a chance he could have, and if he does, then that means I've broken pack law and—"

"Now, hold on here." Willard leaned forward and picked up the bottle, gesturing with it across the table for me to hold out my glass, which I did, so he could fill it. "You said he bit you, right?"

"Yeah." I blushed, knowing I had put myself in a position to be bitten by a human.

"Then you've broken no laws. The law is you can't bite or in any way seek to infect intentionally," Willard said, and Pete smiled at his lover like he'd just told him they were having a baby.

"But still, he may be infected," I said.

"He may, and now it's your responsibility to watch him, and if at all possible, get him here to the compound on the first full moon so you can monitor him. If he changes, then he'll be your cross to bear." Willard's stern look brokered no argument over his pronouncement.

"What does that mean, exactly?"

Pete sighed and took my hand. "He has to be indoctrinated into the way of the pack, and you'll have to bring your case in front of the elders."

"What case?" I'd thought telling the two of them would be the extent of my embarrassment, but telling all the elders in the pack would really suck.

"If he is werewolf, he'll need the protection of the pack, and the only way for a turnt werewolf to get that is to find a mate within the pack." Willard looked at Pete and smiled softly. "It's not as bad as it sounds. It's happened before."

"Yeah, but he's not my bonded mate. It's not the same as you two." Yep, the two guys sitting in the pack leader's doublewide trailer were a bonded pair. In our culture it was a big deal. Only about one percent of all werewolves ever felt the mate bond, and the fact that Willard had found his mate among the humans had brought a huge upheaval to the way the pack had operated ever since. I didn't know all the details as I'd only joined them about five years ago, but I'd heard the stories. Their mating was one of the main reasons I'd been accepted into their strange collection of werewolves that called itself the Outcast pack.

"I'm sure if he was good-looking enough to find his way into your bed, he'll have no trouble finding a mate here if you're not interested," Pete said. He sipped his drink almost daintily, which looked weird after having seen him rip the throat out of a wild boar in his beast form.

"I don't even know the guy. I met him on Grindr, and he seems like the type who will totally freak out over this."

"Oh, he's going to freak out. There's not a single man alive who won't have some issues with not only finding out werewolves are real but that he's now one of them," Willard said sagely.

"But, let's not count our chickens before they hatch. Your job now is to figure out a way to get him here next week for the full moon without telling him why. We can't risk exposing our secret if he's not infected." Pete and Willard exchanged a look that probably held an entire conversation before Pete added, "You know what will happen to him and you if that was to happen."

"I know," I sighed. Maybe death would be preferable to what my future held if Grindr guy turned out to be infected. There was a reason I played up the hick card when I met my hookups. It usually kept them from wanting to have meaningful conversations with me. I was a pretty face and a good fuck but dumb as a box of rocks as far as they were concerned. Now I'd have to try to get the guy to talk to me, and after I'd told him I wasn't interested in anything more than a quick fuck, how was I going to explain my sudden change of attitude?

"You'll figure it out, and like I said, the chances of him being infected are really low. It's something like only point five percent of people who are possibly contaminated that actually get it. The numbers are in your favor." Willard was trying to make me feel better and maybe give me some hope, but I was as pessimistic as fuck by nature and was sure this would end up biting me somewhere other than my neck.

FINDING OUT WHO Grindr guy was turned out to be surprisingly simple. All I had to do was go to Officer Randy Turnball, the resident cop. He lived in a single wide on the north side of the compound with his kid sister. They'd basically been run out of their old pack when it was determined the little sister didn't have the lycanthropy gene. The parents had wanted to give her up for adoption, but Randy was having none of it. At the age of sixteen, he'd taken his nine-year-old sister and run, ending up here where Willard and Pete took them in and raised them until Randy was able to support the two of them on his own.

I hadn't slept for shit, so I looked like death warmed over when I knocked on Randy's door at seven the next morning. I had to wait for him to answer, and then he gave me the strangest look when he found me on his front steps.

"Damian, what a surprise. Do you want to come in?" He was already dressed in his uniform, and I could hear loud music coming from farther inside the mobile home.

"Do you have a few minutes? Pete told me you usually don't leave until eight, but I don't want to hold you up." I needed his help, but it wasn't like we were friends or anything that would make him want to give it to me. Being part of the pack meant he was likely to do what he could for a fellow member, but I knew there were some people who didn't much care for me, and Randy was friends with one of them.

"Sure, come on in. Want a cup of coffee? I got the pot on."

"That would be great, thanks." I followed him inside and sat at the counter that served as both a divider between the kitchen and living room and a table.

"So what brings you by so early?" he asked, as he set a steaming cup in front of me and pushed the sugar and creamer close enough for me to reach.

"I have a situation, and I wondered if maybe you could help me out." Ignoring the extras, I picked up my cup and sipped the hot bitter liquid.

"What sort of situation? I can't fix a DUI if that's what you're aiming at."

"Do I look like the sort who'd get a DUI?" I shouldn't have asked because, of course, I looked exactly like that kind of guy, but I wasn't. "I need to find someone, but the only thing I have to go off is his Grindr profile and the make and model of his car."

Randy raised an eyebrow as I pulled out my phone and pulled up the app so he could look at SweetGuy12's profile. I wasn't sure if it would help, but when Randy snorted, I glared at him, thinking he was making a comment on my taste in men.

"I know who that is." Randy's smirk made me want to lash out at him, but I remembered I needed his help. He had the information, and he didn't even have to do anything to get it.

"How?"

"He works at the DMV. I see him all the time." Randy shrugged like it was no big deal.

"How can you tell from a picture of a chest that it's the same guy?" I wasn't convinced Randy knew the guy from the DMV. Now, if he'd said he'd fucked him and recognized the tiny mole below the guy's belly button, I'd have believed him one hundred percent.

"If you look at the picture a little harder, you can see his face reflected right there." He pointed out the tiny image reflected on the metal surface of an unidentifiable object.

"Wow, I never even noticed that. You have a good eye." I was impressed.

"I am a cop, you know. I'm trained to notice the details. And that guy? His name is Clay Anderson, and as I said, he works at the DMV. He's a grumpy shit who scares the teenagers when they come in to get their permits. You know that class I teach once a week? Every one of the students says he gives them the stink-eye when they pass."

That didn't sound like the shy, stammering guy I'd met the night before, but I wasn't going to question Randy's assertion it was him. I'd drive down to the DMV and check it out for myself. I was sure I could scrounge up something to make it look like I'd simply popped in to stand around for an hour and a half, even when there were only four people in line and as many working the counter.

I stood after gulping the last of my coffee and held my hand out to Randy. "Thanks for the help. That was easier than I thought it was going to be."

He shook my hand. "Is there a reason you want to find him? I mean, you're not going to do anything to him, are you?"

"No, it's a long story, but I'm not looking to go out and beat him up or anything."

"I figured that; still had to ask, though."

He followed me to the door where I thanked him one more time before hopping in my truck and driving to my own stationary mobile home. I didn't spend much time on the compound because I worked construction and lived out of the camper on the back of my truck to save money. I'd finished up a job in Oklahoma and was supposed to start a new one in Texas in a week when they finished erecting the wind towers on the Melland Valley Wind Farm. It would be my last one for the year, and then I'd be home for a couple of months to recharge my batteries. When I worked, I worked seventy, sometimes eighty, hours a week to get the sites closed down on schedule, so I needed some time off in between, and my company gave it to me because they couldn't find a closer like me.

I pushed the door open and wrinkled my nose. The damn kid I paid to look after Stumple and Grumpkin, my two Maine coons, while I was gone, had failed to empty the litter boxes again. I hadn't been home, since the first thing I did when I hit town was look for a hookup, and then I'd passed out in my camper, drunk off my ass after having a bottle of whiskey and listening to Pete and Willard reminisce about their fated romance. I'd have to chew the little shit a new asshole again and dock his pay because this was beyond the pale.

The two huge cats converged on me and wound around my legs, vying for my attention. I reached down and scratched both behind the ears, earning me purrs that sounded like motorcycle engines. Something about the sound of a cat purring calmed my nerves the way nothing else could. I wished I could sit on the floor and cuddle them for a couple of hours, but I had things to do, so I had to settle for a quick snuggle as I picked each one up and hugged them. After changing the litter boxes, I fed the beasts before leaving once again. I had the paperwork for my old boat, and needing new tags for it was the perfect excuse to go to the DMV.

THE DMV ON a Wednesday morning is like the first circle of hell; everyone sits around waiting and looking like they wonder if they'll ever get out, knowing they might not. I took a number from the little red box thing and looked at the screen to see I was ten numbers away from being helped. My gaze traveled over the people working the counter and found all older ladies, no Clay among them. I thought about leaving, but then I spotted a familiar head of black hair poking up from behind a divider in the back of the office. Bingo.

I lounged against the wall as I waited, trying to ignore the looks I got from various people walking in and out of the small office. I knew what most of them thought about guys like me. I could give less fucks about their opinions, but it did get irritating when mothers of small children pulled them as far away from me as they could when they passed. My number was one away when Clay took up a position behind the counter. I cursed under my breath, thinking he'd get the next customer and my wait would have been for nothing.

Sometimes things work in a person's favor, and that morning at the DMV, of all places, it worked in mine. The lady next to Clay punched her button, calling up the next number to her station just before Clay hit his and called up mine. I grinned as I walked to the counter, but then I remembered why I was there and I couldn't maintain it. Clay, on the other hand, looked outright horrified by my presence in his workplace.

"Morning, cupcake," I said, dropping my papers on the counter in front of him. He didn't even glance at them; instead, his mouth dropped open, drawing my attention to it. I still regretted not having the time to get those full pouty lips wrapped around my cock, but this was no time to be thinking about sex. I needed to weasel my way into Clay's life without him knowing I was doing it.

"W-what are you doing here?" Once he regained some of his composure, his hazel glare could have killed me if he'd been able to throw the icicles in it.

"This is the department of motor vehicles, isn't it?" I asked innocently while looking around like I was checking for a sign or something.

"It is." His two words were as frosty as his stare.

"Well, I'm thinking of doing some fishing, and I realized the tags on my boat have expired. This is the place to be if you're in need of renewed tags so you can enjoy some recreational water sports, right?"

Clay's eyes narrowed before he looked at the papers I'd put down. He grunted and put a form in front of me. "Fill that out and sign it." He turned away and started stamping things and stapling other things, making quite the show out of being too busy to chat after I'd filled out all the blanks on the renewal form.

"That'll be thirty-five fifty," he said when he laid my yellow tags on the counter with my renewed registration.

"So, since it seems we're fated to run into each other like this, what do you say I take you out for lunch?" I asked, looking at the clock to make my point that it was almost noon.

"No, and it's still thirty-five fifty for the renewal."

Well, that was cold. I pulled out my wallet but wasn't giving up yet. "Why not? You have to eat, right?"

Clay looked from one side to the other at his coworkers before leaning over the counter toward me. "What's with the way you're talking?" he asked in an angry whisper.

"What do you mean?" I knew exactly what he meant.

"Where's the aw shucks, ain't ya gotta eat? Was last night just an act? Because I was a sure thing, you didn't need to sweet-talk me with your Southern twang to get my pants off," he hissed.

"Hey," I said, holding my hands up in surrender, which only made it look like I was being mugged since I had my wallet in one hand and money in the other, so I quickly put them down before it drew attention to us. "We all play a part when we meet people to hook up. The stupid rube is mine, and the wide-eyed innocent is yours. You don't see me busting your balls about acting like a dick now, do you?"

"Look. Just pay for the registration and go away."

"Just let me—"

"Is there a problem here?" An older lady with bluish-gray hair, and wearing a sweater with a dog on it, came over to see what the fuss was about. The way she looked at Clay made it clear she wasn't too pleased to have him working with her.

"It's nothing, Betty. The customer was having a hard time finding the correct change, but I told him I could break a fifty." Clay eyed the one I was holding in my hand as he held out his to take it.

There was nothing I could do but give him the bill. I didn't want to get him into trouble at work. That would go against my aim of getting him to go out with me. He quickly made change under the watchful eye of the elderly woman before pasting a fake smile on his face as he handed it to me. "Have a nice day and enjoy your *water sports*," he said.

"I will, thanks." Rolling my eyes got me a somewhat real grin from Clay. Well, that was a start, not a good one, but I'd take what I could get. I turned on my heel and went out to sit in my truck. I'd wait and catch him when he left for lunch, and if he stayed in to eat, I'd be there when he finished his shift. I had nowhere to be, and Clay was the only business I needed to attend to. I laid my seat back—maybe I'd nap a bit.

Chapter Three

CLAY

"See you tomorrow, Clay," Betty said when I passed her office at the end of my shift.

"Have a good night, Betty," I called before pushing my way out the heavy steel door leading to the employee parking lot in the back. She got over her little snit earlier when I gave her the piece of cake from my lunch. That little bit of chocolatey goodness was the only thing that kept me going all morning, but after my run-in with Damian, I knew I needed to get her off my back or she'd find a reason to write me up again. She always seemed to have it in for me, but I had no idea why.

I was unlocking my door when a hand landed on my shoulder, making me jump and drop my empty lunch cooler. Turning to face whatever threat approached me, I brought my fist up—keys held between my knuckles—in case I'd need to defend myself. However, I stopped short of actually throwing a punch because it could have been one of my coworkers, and hitting some little old lady I worked with would be bad form. I was sorry I didn't follow through, though, when I saw who was standing there with that shit-eating grin that made me want to knock out his teeth. I dropped my hand instead.

"Don't hit me, cupcake. I promise not to mug you." His grin turned into a smile as he took a step closer, picked up my cooler, and held it out to me. "Do you always try to punch people who come up behind you?"

"Only jerks who I hate," I said, grabbing my cooler out of his hand before turning away to use my keys for what they were intended.

"What did I do to make you hate me so much?"

Did I hear him right? I turned around once again to make sure he wasn't pulling my leg with another one of his acts. "What did you do to me?"

"Yeah, last I knew, we had a good time, and the only thing I said was that I didn't want anything more than a hookup, which if I'm not mistaken, is exactly why most guys use Grindr. Why are you so pissed at me?"

"Do you not remember last night in your truck when I told you I might have swallowed your blood and you freaked out? Why don't you tell me what *you did* to me, huh?" Yeah, if he thought I was going to forget his reaction, he was sorely mistaken. I'd already called to make an appointment at the clinic on my lunch break the next day. I hoped it was something they could detect right away and not something that would lurk in my system, only to come back and bite me a month or two down the road.

"I told you, I didn't think it was a good idea to be drinking someone's blood—not like you're a vampire, right?" he asked as if it were all some joke.

"Why don't you go the fuck away? I mean, if you can only make jokes about stupid made-up creatures, you're not worth any more of my time." This time I didn't wait for him to try to explain himself. I opened my door and got in, locking it right after I slammed it in his face.

He knocked on my window. Even though I didn't roll it down, I still heard his words through the glass. "You're the one who bit me. Remember that." He turned and strode off after leaving me with that little tidbit to mull over.

IT TOOK ME exactly twenty-three minutes to drive from the office to my house. I lived in a town that was not officially a town. Shit, the name of the place was Grebes, but everyone called it Grebes Village. It was a tiny place that had sprung up in the middle of nowhere to serve the summer lake people. There's a community center with a small library, a gas station that also serves as a bait shop and still rents the occasional DVD, a liquor store, and of course, the Grebes Pub, which is also a restaurant and known simply as the Pub. The rest of the town consists of twenty houses loosely grouped around the two intersecting highways.

I parked in my driveway and stared at my little one-and-a-half-story house. It needed a coat of paint, but it was in good shape. My parents had died the summer I was supposed to go off to college, leaving me the house but no desire to seek the college education they'd insisted I needed. My best friend's dad—my ex-best friend because Jon had gone off to college and moved to the city afterward—had gotten me the job at the DMV because he felt bad for the poor orphan boy. I'd worked there for almost ten years now, and I was happy with my life, for the most part.

My nights usually consisted of heating up some sort of leftovers from meals I'd made over the weekend or the carryout I'd stopped and picked up on the way home. Tonight, I was having reheated tuna casserole with a side of wontons, which I ate in front of the television. I was trying not to think about Damian, but my mind kept going back to him asking me out to lunch. Why had he wanted to go out with me when he'd had no interest in even learning my name after we'd fucked? It was a mystery, so I decided I wanted nothing to do with the guy. He wasn't my type anyway. I snorted. At this point, my type was male and having a heartbeat, but still, something about Damian rubbed me the wrong way.

I browsed the Internet for a bit and checked my Grindr app, but shut it down as soon as MoonGazer popped up as online. And then I showered and went to bed.

THE SECOND FRIDAY night of the month was all-you-can-eat walleye at the Grebes Pub, and it was the one time I braved the crowds to eat there. I loved me some walleye and felt like I should celebrate my semiclean bill of health. There were a couple of tests I was still waiting for, but my doctor was fairly certain I could cease my worry over a few of them since they weren't all that common. The only one I had to worry about was the HIV test that I couldn't even take for another couple of weeks. And though I did worry about it some, Damian seemed like the kind of guy who would have told me if he knew he had it. I don't know why I came to that conclusion about him, especially since he'd lied to me before, but it was a feeling I got and it eased my mind a little.

Jenny, the hostess slash head waitress, seated me at one of the small tables near the back of the pub after she asked me if anyone would be joining me—to which I rolled my eyes because she knew better. I was as good as the town hermit because, after my parents died, I couldn't form the kind of bond with people that would put me at risk of going through the loss again. I'd shunned my friends until they left me alone, and I never bothered to make new ones.

I ordered tap beer and the special. There was some background music playing, but it wasn't so loud that it hindered conversation—not that I was going to hold one with myself, but I could have if I wanted to. I pulled out my phone and tried to pass the time until my food arrived by scrolling through a few of my favorite forums on Reddit. I was in the middle of reading a horror story about a bunch of kids in a trailer in the woods when the chair on the other side of my table was pulled out. I didn't look up because usually everyone knew I ate alone, and it wasn't unusual for someone to grab my extra chair to add another seat to their table.

"So, you find a new guy for tonight, or are you still looking?"

My head snapped up at the sound of Damian's voice. He was sitting at my table, arms resting on the top as he leaned forward to look at me.

"I'm not online tonight, but I am right here if you want to chat, or maybe we could go to my camper again?" He raised an eyebrow as if it were a real question that had any possibility of me saying yes.

"Fuck off. What are you doing here?" I'd lived there all my life, and though lots of people came through in the summer, in the off season, I knew every single person in town, and I'd never seen Damian at the Pub before.

"I heard they had excellent walleye here, and it's all you can eat tonight. I'm hungry, so I decided to stop in and see for myself what the fuss was all about, and imagine my surprise when I saw you sitting here all by yourself. I thought, why not go join him? So here I am." Damian shrugged like his story made one lick of sense, but I wasn't buying it.

"I thought that's why you registered your boat, so you could catch your own fish." I reminded him of the last time we'd seen each other and the reason for it.

"Well, I can eat a lot, and I'd have to fish for hours if I wanted an all-I-can-eat buffet of those suckers. And that's only if I was lucky enough for them to be biting."

"So, you've never been in here before?" I asked because it didn't seem to trip him up when I asked about his boat and supposed fishing excursion he needed to take. He shook his head in answer to my question. "And you just happened to wander in tonight?" He nodded. "The one night of the month I come here to eat?" He grinned and shrugged again as if it was the world's greatest coincidence. "I call bullshit."

"You can believe what you want, but it's the truth."

"Where are you from?" I thought I'd try a different tack and see if I could find something about him that might help me figure out what I was dealing with when it came to Damian Maccon.

"A little place outside Pelican. You probably wouldn't know of it," he said, sitting back in his chair, seemingly relaxed when faced with personal questions.

"Try me. I grew up here. I know every town from here to the cities," I said, pretty confident I could pinpoint any town he named on the map, no matter the size.

"It's not an official town."

I raised my hands to indicate the place we were sitting. "Neither is Grebes, but here we are."

He shifted to cross his legs, one ankle resting on the other knee. "It's called Thylacine, but it's not on any maps."

"So you're from a town that doesn't exist. Makes sense," I said. Seeing Jenny approaching from behind Damian, I tried to warn her off with my eyes, hoping to avoid having to explain my unexpected dining companion. I also wanted to stop him from ordering food and making it harder to get rid of him, but Jenny didn't get the signal.

"Hi there. What can I get for you tonight?" she asked Damian, but her eyes were locked on my face, which was getting hotter by the second under both of their stares.

"I'll have what he's having, assuming he's not stupid and ordered the walleye." Damian pulled his gaze off me and trained it on Jenny, who finally had enough of trying to read my mind with her eyes and looked at the stranger sitting before her. She turned even redder than I probably was when he gave her his sexy grin and a wink to push it over the top.

Jenny giggled. "He ordered the walleye. Even Clay isn't that stupid. You want a beer too?"

"Sure do, thanks." Damian let his smile brighten her night for another five seconds before turning back to me. "She has a high opinion of you."

"She always has," I said. "So you intend on staying for supper then?"

"That's what I came here for."

I had a hard time believing that, but I wasn't self-absorbed enough to think he'd go out of his way to track me down, not once, but twice. It had to have been a coincidence, no matter how much I wanted to read more into it. Not that I was keen on having a stalker, but it was strange that he'd shown up twice in the past three days when I'd never seen him before that night in the camper.

"I guess it would be rude to make you leave after you ordered, but don't get any funny ideas. I'm going home alone after I eat."

"Suit yourself," he said, and I thought that would end the weirdness, but then what he asked next raised the hairs on the back of my neck. "So did that doctor give you a clean bill of health, or what?"

"Here's your beer, and your fish will be out in a couple of minutes," Jenny said as she put a frosted mug on the table. She didn't notice we were in the middle of the tensest stare down ever and left when neither of us did more than bob our head in response.

"H-how did you know I went to the doctor?" He was stalking me! What sort of weirdo stalks their Grindr hookup after telling them... Ugh, why was he so weird?

"Ah, there's that stutter I love so much," he said, like him freaking me the fuck out was funny.

"Answer the question."

"I didn't know you went to the doctor, but you said you were going and you seem like the sort of guy who does what he says he's going to do, so I assumed you had."

Again, his answer made perfect sense, but I got the feeling he was lying to me. I guess I really didn't trust him not to lie to my face. "It's really none of your business, but if you must know, the tests he could take right away came back negative."

"I told you I was clean. And I can see you're still worried about the big one and I can tell you that I don't have HIV, so you can relax." He picked up his beer and tipped it to me in a sort of salute before taking a drink.

"And why should I believe you? You're just some random fuck who all of a sudden keeps showing up where you have no business being, and let's not forget the whole hick act that you pulled on me. It's not like you're the most honest person I've ever met." With that, I picked up my beer and mimicked his actions.

"I do that exaggerated accent and shit because it keeps guys like you from thinking they might want a second go-round with me. Tell me you really wanted to get to know me better when you thought I was some uneducated redneck who lived in a camper."

So he had a point, but it didn't mean I had to like being lied to.

"See, and that's why I do it." His grin turned into a smirk at his win.

"What do you mean by guys like me?" It was bugging me because, though I knew I was no prize, I also knew I wasn't disgusting or anything. I didn't think I should be lumped into a category like that with the other losers.

Damian dropped his leg and sat forward once again. "You're lonely. I can smell it on you. Lonely guys get clingy and I don't do clingy."

Before I could refute his claim, Jenny showed up with our plates. She tried to get Damian's attention again, but he ignored her in favor of his food. I put lemon on mine while he used tartar sauce, which made me cringe. Why order great fish and then cover up the taste of it with that white goop? I didn't ask and I doubt I'd have gotten an answer because Damian devoured his food like it was either his first meal after a fast or his last before death. I was fascinated by the way he ate, and he had his second plate in front of him before I'd even finished half of my first because I was too busy watching him to eat my own meal.

"What? You don't like the fish?" he asked when he noticed I wasn't gobbling mine down like he was.

"No, it's good, but I don't eat like you do. I prefer to chew my food, not wolf it down like a dog."

His head popped up and he stared at me. I swear I heard a low growl come from him, but then he smiled. "Grew up in a big family—if I didn't eat fast, I went hungry."

"Okay, I guess that would explain it, but do you think you can slow down a bit? I keep waiting for you to choke on a fish bone and it's making me tense." And to be honest, I was a little embarrassed to be seen with someone who ate like a pig in public. He would be the talk of the town for the next month if he kept at it like he was.

"I can try, but I make no promises." He dove back in as I shook my head and tried to look around to see who was watching without looking like I was doing just that.

He consumed three more plates, and I had one additional helping. Jenny was busy, so our table looked like a fish graveyard by the time she came to take some of the plates away. I was pleasantly full, and all I wanted to do was go home and veg in front of the television.

"So, what are we going to do next?" Damian asked. He finished off his beer—I think it was his seventh or eighth—I'd lost count because he drank like he ate: fast and sloppily.

"Well, I'm going to go home and watch some Netflix. I have no idea what's on your itinerary." I wanted to make it crystal clear I wasn't going to spend another minute with him now that I wasn't under social pressure to do so. Once we left the Pub, I was free to make a scene if he didn't leave quietly.

"Aw, you're no fun. Let's go do something."

"No, thanks."

"Why not?"

"Because I don't like you, and therefore I don't want to spend time with you. Is that clear enough for you?" I asked as I stood.

"That's pretty harsh. I was only trying to be friendly." He stood too, and it was then I realized he wasn't as tall as I remembered him to be. Standing so close it was easy to see he had only an inch or two on me. Funny, he was much bigger in my memory. The tattoo on his neck was the same, and that's when I noticed something strange. "What are you staring at?"

"Where's the bite mark?" There should have been a set of teeth marks on him if I'd bitten hard enough to draw blood.

"It's there, but it's hard to see because of the ink," he said, but he put his hand up to cover the blemish-free spot of skin.

"No, I'm pretty sure I'd be able to see it, and there's nothing there." I stepped closer, but he stepped back away from me, making me suspicious and wanting to see his neck even more. "Why are you hiding it from me?"

"I'm not." He looked at his wrist and said, "Oh, look at the time. I really should be going."

"You're not wearing a watch," I pointed out, but he'd already turned and made his way to the front of the pub. I grabbed my jacket, intending to catch up to him, but I got caught walking upstream against a huge party that was being seated in my area, and by the time I made it to the front, he was gone. I went to the register to pay for my meal and probably his too since he'd left so fast.

"Your friend already paid the tab. Left a pretty good tip too. Told me to tell you that you owed him one and he'd catch up with you later to collect." Jenny was grinning from ear to ear at having delivered the message that she probably thought had deeper meaning.

"Yeah, I'm sure he will. Have a good night." I walked out into the chilly evening and looked around to see if Damian's truck was in the lot, but it wasn't. Neither was my car, but I'd walked since I knew I was going to have a few beers, which reminded me of how much Damian had drank. I briefly worried about him driving after he'd had so much but then decided I didn't care. It was his life, and it meant nothing to me.

Chapter Four

DAMIAN

I failed. Having given up on the idea that I'd be able to lure Clay to the compound with the promise of a hot night of sex, I had to focus on another way to get him there. I'd convinced myself that since it was for his own well-being, I would use force if necessary. I was on my own because no one in the pack wanted to risk exposure if Clay wasn't infected. I understood it was my responsibility and didn't hold it against any of the handful of guys I'd approached to ask for help when they declined but politely offered me suggestions on how to knock someone out without causing lasting damage.

I'd been tailing Clay around for a few days. At first I thought he might have suspected I was doing it, because he kept looking around like he could feel someone watching him. I don't think he saw me, though, because it would have been just like him to call me out if he had. I felt confident that I went undetected as I followed him through his boring routine.

When the night before the full moon arrived, I followed him home from the Blue Moon where he'd been hit on several times but had turned down every man and went home alone. It made me wonder about him. I knew from our brief encounters that he didn't think much of himself, but once I'd gotten him in bed, he didn't fail to deliver. I'd been afraid he was a timid bottom, and though I liked topping, I got thrust into that role more often than not, so it was nice to find a guy who didn't automatically assume I was opposed to catching. Or worse yet, refuse to top me because they didn't feel they could.

Parking a few feet from the end of his driveway, where I was concealed by a line of bushes, I settled in to wait a couple of hours to give him enough time to go to bed and hopefully fall asleep. I'd been there earlier and made sure I could easily get in without making too much noise. His house had a basement, and I'd only had to exert a little bit of pressure on one of the small windows to pop it open. I was fairly certain he wouldn't notice it was ajar if he made a trip down the stairs.

I pulled out my phone and played a few games to pass the time as I watched for his lights to go off. It took longer than I'd hoped for the light in the bay window in the front of the house to go out and the one in the window on the top floor to turn on. If he followed his nightly routine, he'd be in bed with the lights off in less than twenty minutes. I'd give him another hour before I'd go in. I needed Clay sleeping and disoriented if I wanted to pull off getting him blindfolded and subdued without him seeing me.

If I knew for sure he'd caught the lycanthropy virus, I'd have simply gone in, not caring, but if he ended up not having it, I'd be in a shit ton of hot water for kidnapping the guy. It was the major sticking point in my plan. I'd waffled between waiting until the last moment to snatch him and doing it the way I was currently set to do it, which was to take him and hold him for the day at my place on the compound. I couldn't take the chance that he'd veer from his routine and I'd miss out on my opportunity because he decided to drive into the city for a movie or some other dumb shit.

Adrenaline made my wolf want to come out, but I was old enough I could keep it at bay, even when I was standing over Clay's sleeping form and so jacked my heart felt like it was going to burst out of my chest. I'd never been on the wrong side of the law before in such a huge way. I'd gotten a few speeding tickets and been hauled in to the station for fighting a couple of times, but I'd never committed a felony. The feeling I got preparing to do it made me realize why people could get addicted to crime, even though they knew the consequences if they got caught.

Pulling the blindfold out of my pocket, I eased my way onto Clay's bed so I was next to him but slightly higher on the mattress. I needed to be able to get my arm around his neck and have the leverage to apply enough pressure to knock him out. I was thankful for my enhanced reflexes when he unexpectedly rolled toward me, and I had to shift away from him. A small moan issued from his lips and went straight to my cock, but I tamped down the temptation of a mostly naked and invitingly sleep-warmed Clay.

Taking a deep breath to center myself again, I made my move. With lightning-quick strikes, I shoved the blindfold over his head and wrapped my right arm around his neck, while my left went behind his head. I lifted him so that he sat in the cradle of my thighs, giving me the leverage to squeeze just enough to cut off the blood supply to his brain. He didn't even have the time to struggle before his body went limp in my arms not more than ten seconds later.

With the hard part out of the way, I bundled Clay into his blanket and hefted him over my shoulder, glad for the extra strength my genetics gave me. I accidently knocked his head on the wall when I turned to go down the stairs, but otherwise all went well. The deserted street of a small town was the only witness to my crime as I carried him to the camper on the back of my truck.

Once inside, I put him on the floor so I wouldn't have to worry about him falling off something as I drove back to the compound. Not one to skimp on precautions, I handcuffed his feet to the metal bars by the door and his hands to the post that held up the tiny table, giving him no wiggle room if he were to wake before we made it to my trailer. Last thing I needed was to have gone through the trouble of abducting him without him seeing me to have him take the blindfold off if he awoke before I reckoned he should.

I drove the speed limit down the highway before turning off on the dirt road leading to the compound. The pack's land was mostly forested, with the settlement built on the shore of a small lake in the center. My trailer was at the far end of the encampment with its own little slice of beach. I backed into my driveway and got out.

My closest neighbor's house was about five hundred feet away, and the guy who lived there, Mark, was sitting on his front porch looking up at the almost-full moon. The moon had that sort of pull on all of us when it was so close to full, but I resisted the urge to look up because I knew I could stand there hypnotized for an hour if I did. Mark didn't even acknowledge me, but I wasn't worried if he suddenly decided to pay attention to what I was doing. On the compound, the rule was you minded your business, and unless something was happening that was going to affect the pack, you kept what you saw to yourself. Plus, pretty much everyone knew what I was going to be up to with Clay all weekend, and most of them wanted no part of it. I'd have plenty of privacy.

Clay wasn't moving when I opened the camper door, so I suspected he was still passed out, but that changed when I released his first foot. I had to dodge the kick that would have hit me squarely in the jaw if it had connected.

"Help! Help! Someone help!" Clay started screaming and squirming while I tried to get him uncuffed from his moorings. He kicked and hollered and then tried to punch me with his linked-together hands when they were released from the chain holding them to the metal post. I had no choice other than to try to subdue him again, but getting him in the sleeper hold was much harder when he was awake and fighting for his life.

I bit my tongue to keep from saying something to try to calm him. He'd recognize my voice by now, so I had to fight his panic in silence. When I finally got a good hold on him and was about to choke him into submission again, his voice lowered from a scream level to almost a whisper as he asked, "Why are you doing this to me?"

I couldn't answer him, and thankfully, I didn't have to because he finally slipped into unconsciousness again.

"That looked exhausting." Mark had come to watch the fun and was grinning at me through the open camper door. "He's got a strong will that will serve him well if he's infected."

"Yeah, there's that, I guess," I mumbled as I dragged Clay's limp body out of my camper and threw him over my shoulder again.

"If you need anything, give a holler," Mark said before walking off, eyes skyward once more.

"Sure thing, thanks." I knew the offer was only a polite gesture because until Clay turned, or didn't, I was on my own.

Placing Clay on my bed, I undid the handcuffs so I could chain him back up spread-eagle in the middle of the mattress. Once that was done, I threw his blanket over him and went to get myself a drink.

I was four shots in when my phone rang. I answered it only because it was Pete; anyone else I would have ignored. "Hello?"

"I saw you drive in a while ago, so I wanted to check in and see if you'd gotten the task done and if you needed anything." Pete sounded like he was trying to keep his voice low, and I wondered if Willard knew he was calling to offer his help.

"I got him here. He's secured and I think I have everything I need, but I'll make sure you're the one I call if I don't."

His soft chuckle came down the line, reminding me of how much I liked the old man and how much I owed him and Willard for taking me in when I had nowhere else to go. "You know my story, so I'd expect nothing less. If he changes, make sure I'm the first one you call. Try not to drink yourself to death tonight and get some sleep."

"I won't and I'll try. Thanks for calling, Pete."

"It's nothing to let you know someone has your back, just common courtesy. Good night, son."

"Good night." I put my phone on the table and stared at it. I'd been lucky the day I'd run into Pete. He was more of a father to me than my own had ever been. I hoped I wouldn't do something that ended up with him having to put me out, but as my eyes went to my bedroom door, I got the feeling Clay would be my downfall.

WAKING UP TO screaming when you've got a hangover is not the best way to start a morning. I rolled over and pulled one of the couch cushions over my head, but it did fuck-all to drown out the racket Clay was making. Frustrated, I threw the pillow across the room and got up. I stumbled down the hall to the bathroom and took a handful of pills while I pissed before going to see my captive.

I put my hand over my mouth to stifle my laughter when I took in the scene before me. Stumple and Grumpkin were on the bed, one on each side of Clay. Stumple was lapping at Clay's neck while Grumpkin was kneading his side with his paws. I clapped my hands to get their attention, but they ignored me, which was par for the course with the two of them. Picking Stumple up from the bed got Grumpkin's attention, and he followed when I carried his brother out of the room.

"You two are bad," I whispered to my two big cats, but I couldn't help chuckling. I wondered what Clay was thinking, lying there blind and being molested by two huge felines must have put some very strange ideas about what was to come into his head. I put the cats in their outside pen, thinking it was probably best to keep them away from Clay for the time being.

Clay had stopped screaming and therefore heard when I entered the room again. I could tell because his head turned to the doorway and he cocked it as if he was trying to hear better. "Who are you, and what are you going to do to me?" he asked when enough time had passed and he probably figured out I wasn't going to speak. "You can let me go, and I promise I won't go to the cops. Please, just let me go." His words trailed off into a whimper, and I thought for sure he was going to start crying, but his jaw clenched instead.

He rattled his chains and shook the bed as he struggled. "You crazy fucker, let me go, or so help me god—" I shut the door and left him to rant to himself. I smiled a little, though. Clay was tougher than I'd given him credit for. If our situations had been reversed, I'm not sure I could have kept from sobbing and begging for mercy. His anger, though mildly surprising considering the predicament he found himself in, fit with his personality.

After puttering around the kitchen for a bit, I made coffee and a big greasy breakfast for myself, which I ate before making Clay a bacon and egg sandwich. I poured him a glass of orange juice, figuring the hot coffee wasn't such a good idea.

He was lying still, but I could hear his breathing as it sped up when he heard me step into the room. I could also smell the ripe pungent odor of his fear wafting up off him in tantalizing waves. My wolf growled, making my chest rumble with the sound I couldn't control.

"I heard that!" Clay lifted his head and swiveled it around, finally pinning his blinded eyes in my direction. God, I wished I could say something. Every fiber in my being wanted to snap out a sharp retort, but I bit it back. I was going to check it out and see if I could find a phone app that would disguise my voice after I was done feeding Clay his breakfast. It would give me something to pass the time, and if I was successful, I could tell Clay to calm down and that nothing bad was going to happen to him.

Placing the plate on the nightstand, I sat on the edge of the bed. Clay tried to shift away, but his bindings didn't allow for much movement. I reached out to cup the back of his head, but he jerked violently away from me. How the hell was I supposed to relay the fact that I was only going to try to give him a drink when I couldn't talk? I should have planned better for this.

Inspiration hit, and I put the glass down and picked up the sandwich instead. I held it out and then slowly inched toward his face so it ended up under his nose where he could smell it and know what my intentions were. It didn't make much of a difference, though, because he shook his head and pursed his lips tightly together until I moved the food away.

"I'm not eating anything from you, you fucking nutcase."

Guess I should have seen that coming. I got up but left the food on the nightstand. Maybe the aroma would make him hungry enough to eat when I came back at lunchtime. I walked to the door, but Clay's voice stopped me in my tracks.

"Damian?" His voice was unsure as he said my name, but now there was no doubt in my mind he suspected I was the one who'd grabbed him. I didn't answer, even to deny it was me because that would have only confirmed it for him. "If that's you, Damian, I'm sorry. I'm sorry I was such an asshole to you, and I didn't mean it. I don't hate you, so if that's why you're doing this, you don't have to. I like you. I really, really like you, so please, let me loose and we can talk it over. I swear, I won't hold this against you if you let me go right now."

I shook my head. He was some sort of evil bastard. Thinking I'd be dumb enough to fall for that story. The dude was seriously fucked in the head, says the guy who's currently got another chained to his bed. I left him there because I couldn't provide any comfort, so staying in the room with him probably only caused him more anxiety than being alone with his thoughts.

I grabbed a beer and took it out onto the back deck. It was chilly out but not so cold that there was frost in the mornings or that I needed a coat for a walk down to the dock, where I sat at the end with my legs swinging out over the water. I had time to think and wondered if this would be one of those life-changing events that would mean I'd have to run again. The thought made me sad. I'd lived with the Outcast pack for just under five years, but it felt more like home than home did. I'd surely hate to have to move on because I'd had to land the Grindr fish that kept getting away.

It's true what they said. A man's cock really could get him into more trouble than anything else.

Chapter Five

CLAY

The door shut, and I knew I was alone again. After the initial shock of having woken up blindfolded and bound, I'd been able to calm down enough to assess my situation. Concluding that I was completely and utterly fucked didn't stop me from spending a good part of the night testing the bonds holding me to the bed. I was sure there was no getting out of the leather cuffs hooked to a chain that I figured was attached to the bed I was lying on.

Once that was done, I turned my mind to trying to figure out what the fuck had caused me to end up chained to the bed in the first place. My life was so boring it took me about three minutes to hone in on the only thing that had changed in the recent days. Damian. The name pulled up a picture of the sexy but infuriating man who grinned entirely too much for my liking.

He was the only explanation for this fucked-up mess I found myself in. Only thing I'd yet to figure out was why he'd kidnap me. My mind supplied me with all sorts of scenarios that weren't helpful when I was trying to remain calm. Even having some sort of animal—I was guessing cats, but the size and the way they purred had me imagining baby tigers or something—licking me hadn't done more to freak me out than my own deranged fantasies.

Time surely passed, but not being able to see and being forced to lie there, I could only judge the passage by the way my stomach started rumbling. Suddenly, I was cursing myself for refusing the food the man—Damian, fucker—had offered. Then I was thirsty, but soon, food and drink were the least of my worries and the pressure in my bladder made me do the last thing on earth I wanted to do.

"I need to piss!" I screamed as loud as my parched throat would allow. When the door didn't open soon enough for me to think the guy had heard me, I tried again. "Come on, fucker! I need to piss now!"

He must have already been on his way because the door opened and I could hear him walking toward the bed. Maybe I'd get a chance to escape when he let me up to use the bathroom. I started mentally preparing for the fight to come, but as quickly as the thought had entered my mind, it left. That sick fucker pulled the front of my boxer briefs down, and his chilly hand grabbed my cock.

"Urinate now." A robotic voice gave the instruction, and before I could even comprehend what was going on, I let go.

"Oh, fuck, that feels like heaven," I groaned as my bladder emptied. The sound of liquid filling a bottle told me of the fucker's ingenious solution to my problem. By making me use a bottle, he didn't have to risk me fighting him to save himself the cleanup if I pissed in the bed. I finished pissing, and he pulled my shorts back up. "Thanks." I figured it couldn't hurt to be a little polite, even if I felt the bile rise when I said the word. I wouldn't have to thank him for letting me pee if he hadn't chained me to the goddamn bed! I could still rant in my head; there was that at least.

He grunted, and the sounds told me he was leaving again. "Wait!" The footsteps halted and then came back toward the bed. "I'm thirsty. Can I have some water, please?"

"Orange juice," the robot voice said again.

"Fine, anything; my throat is killing me." I opened my mouth, but nothing filled it.

"Stop screaming, bad for throat."

"Fuck you, robot voice. You'd scream too if you were being held by a lunatic!" I shouted. The chuckle was not robotic, and it confirmed the person in the room with me was Damian. I was about to say so, but this time when I opened my mouth, the rim of a glass hit my lip, giving me just enough warning to not choke to death on the fluid flowing into my mouth. A hand cupped the back of my head, supporting it as I drained the glass. Peeing felt like heaven, and the juice was a close second.

"Food."

"You know, I know it's you, Damian. It wouldn't take a genius to figure it out," I said when he used the stupid computer-generated voice once again.

"Food."

"Ugh, why are you doing this?" I was so frustrated and beyond caring any longer. "If you're going to kill me, why not just get it over with?" Seriously, if he was going to kill me, and let's be honest, what else could he possibly have planned for me? He may as well get on with it.

"Food."

"Fuck!" He was so infuriating! "Fine, give me the fucking food, you delusional fucktard."

He snorted but then shoved something in my mouth. I was half expecting it to be a gag, but nope, it was a soggy sandwich. I didn't care. I took a huge bite and then gobbled down the rest of it as the hand fed it to me.

"Drink."

"Yes, I'd like one." Back to being sort of polite. I could only hope Damian was probably playing out some sick, twisted fantasy, and he'd get tired of it soon and let me go. Hey, a guy who's tied to a bed with no hope of escape can dream, right?

This time, it was a bottle of water that he held to my lips after he grabbed my head and tilted it up. I chugged most of it even though it would mean another date with the bottle at my dick later. "Thanks." I turned my head to wipe my mouth on the pillow below me once he let go of my head. "Do you have a plan? Like are you going to torture me first or maybe make me lay here until you get up the nerve to kill me?"

His breath in my face was a surprise but not as big of one as the hand that ran down my chest and ended up cupping my package. A whole new set of nightmares flashed through my mind. What if he was going to rape me to death? A cold sweat covered my body, and he snuffled at my neck in a way that was so familiar my cock started to get hard just thinking about the last—the only—time I'd fucked Damian. He chuckled as he pulled away, but he still didn't talk to me.

"You're a sick bastard, you know that?"

The only answer he gave me was the sound of the door closing as he left me alone once again. Fuck, knowing Damian was my captor was doing nothing to ease my mind. I knew I should have trusted my gut when I got the feeling someone was following me around all week. Maybe if I'd been more vigilant, I could have avoided all this. It was too late now, and the only thing I could do was try to think of a way to convince him to let me go. But maybe a nap first since I'd barely slept all night.

"AH FUCK!" IT hurt so bad. I was out of my mind and in agony. It felt like my body was being turned inside out as the pain ripped through my core.

"Shh, it's okay," Damian whispered into my ear, running a hand down my sweaty face as he did.

"No! Make it stop, please, stop," I whimpered and begged for it to end.

"You'll be fine. Try to relax and let it flow through you, instead of trying to fight it." Damian stared down at me with concern in his mismatched eyes.

I couldn't remember when he'd taken the blindfold off, or when he'd unlocked the leather cuffs from my arms and legs, but I was free to curl up into a ball, and I did exactly that once the pain had gotten so bad it made me throw up. Damian cleaned up the mess the best he could and then resumed his position at my side, petting me and shushing me like I was a child. He kept telling me to embrace the beast. I had no idea what that meant, but fuck that shit; I wasn't embracing anything in the state I was in.

"You have to let it take over. The more you fight against it, the more it will hurt and the longer it will take. Relax and breathe, Clay."

"Fuck you and the horse you rode in on!"

"You're going to regret those words once this is over and I beat your ass for being such a pain in mine." He glared at me, but I could see he was worried.

"If I, ah, fuck, remember, motherfucking, cocksucking bitch, you liked, urgh fuck, fuck, fuck, what I did, goddamn fucksicle to your ass!" Having got out my retort, I clenched into a tighter ball and screamed mindlessly into the pillow.

"Leave it to you to have to get that in even when you're hurting so bad you can barely speak." Damian patted my back, but then he was quiet while I writhed in pain.

Something was itching at the back of my brain, and when I focused on that sensation, the pain eased a little. I'm no dummy, so I concentrated on that niggling little itch and then suddenly I was pain free. I turned to tell Damian the pain had suddenly disappeared, and that's when I noticed something was odd about my eyesight. Holy fucksticks! The pain had probably given me a stroke, and now I was practically color blind.

Damian sat up on the bed and smiled—an actual genuine smile—down at me. "See, I told you it wouldn't be so bad, didn't I?"

I opened my mouth and said, "Woof." No, wait that wasn't what I was trying to say. I did it again, and again I said, "Woof."

"You are completely adorable in that form. I gotta say I didn't expect you to be so damn cute," Damian said as he reached out and patted my head, which was a bit odd. "That bark is a little sad, though. Gonna have to work on that, pup."

Great, a new nickname; *pup* was as bad as *cupcake*. Of course, when I tried to tell him that, it came out as *woof*. What the fuck was wrong with me? Could a stroke affect someone's speech so it was only possible to say *woof*? Something behind me flicked in the corner of my fucked-up vision, and my thoughts went haywire. *Get it*, was the predominate thought, so I tried to do just that. The thought was so repetitive that it took me getting dizzy and falling on the bed for it to register that what I was chasing was a tail. A furry tail that was—and fuck me, I knew it sounded crazy— on my ass. I looked out over the room, and there, over the dresser, was a mirror where I could see myself—or more accurately, I could see the small puppy sitting where I should have been sitting and where my eyes were looking out.

"It's okay, Clay. Don't get too excited. I can explain everything," Damian said when I started ranting at him, but it only came out as yips, yaps, woofs, and barks. He stood and I had to crane my neck to look up at him, but then he bent over and we were face-to-face for a second before he picked me up.

"Put me down, you big dumb ass," is what I tried to say, but of course, that's not what came out of my mouth.

"Calm down, pup. Let's get you out of this room. Are you hungry? I bet you are. Let's see if we can find you something good to eat, huh?" Damian was talking to me in that tone people reserved for babies and tiny animals, which annoyed the fuck out of me. I wriggled, but there was no way I was getting out of his grasp unless he wanted me to.

I had no choice but to watch the walls go by as he carried me through a dark paneled hallway and into an open area that had a living room and kitchen. He set me down on the floor, and that's when the disorientation hit me. I was tiny and the world looked huge. I lay down and did the only thing I could think of to get my feelings across to Damian, who was rummaging in the cupboard: I whined.

"I know, pup, I know it's weird, and I wish I could have told you what to expect, but I couldn't expose the pack without knowing for sure if you'd been infected. Ah-ha, I found it. I knew I had a can of this stocked away somewhere." He came over, set a bowl in front of me, and then opened a can and dumped it into the bowl. "There you go, eat up and then I'll call some friends. We'll go over to meet them, and then we'll go for a run. How's that sound?"

It sounded like fucking bullshit to me, and did he really expect me to eat dog food? I yipped at him, but then the scent of the food from the bowl hit my nose and damn if it didn't smell like the best thing ever. Once again that voice in my head that wasn't my voice started to chant. *Food, food, food, eat it, eat it, eat it, hurry, hurry, hurry.* Next thing I knew, my face was buried in the bowl, and I was *wolfing* down the chunks with barely a thought for chewing them first.

"That's a good boy." Damian patted my head again, then laughed when I growled at him. He got up, and soon a second bowl—this one filled with water—joined the first. By this time my brain was back to being mine, but I was thirsty so I drank the water. "I'm going to make a couple of calls. You go ahead and explore if you want." Damian scratched me behind the ears before getting up and leaving me alone in the new bigger-than-usual world.

I had to be hallucinating. This was not real. Maybe it was a dream brought on by the stress of having been kidnapped and tied to the bed. Had to be, right? There was no way I was currently looking at my reflection in the metal trash can—a small black-and-white puppy with hazel eyes. I looked a little like one of those wolves, but not quite like a domesticated one. What were they called? I knew this. It was a husky or something, maybe a malamute? Ah, who cared what fucking breed of dog I was? I was a fucking dog! Seriously, this had to be a dream, so I'd let it play out, and hopefully, I'd wake up and everything would be back to normal. That was, if you could call being chained to a bed in a crazy man's house normal.

Walking on four feet seemed to come naturally, so I did as Damian suggested and wandered around the room. Other natural doggy instincts took over from time to time. The need to sniff everything was one that bugged me because I stuck my nose in every little crevasse I could find, and I was unable to stop myself from doing it. There was one scent that caught my attention because it was all over the house, and it stuck out from Damian's. I sniffed my way across the room to the glass door leading out to a small deck and jumped back when a huge cat stared back at me and then another joined it.

The urge to bark was simply too great, and I did just that. In my head, the word *bark* repeated over and over, but what came out of my mouth didn't sound like the word in my head. Both cats arched their backs and hissed at me through the door. I was glad the glass was between us, because no matter how brave my inner dog was, I was scared shitless of those monster-sized felines.

Once again, the world shifted as Damian scooped me up into his arms. "I see you've met Stumple and Grumpkin. They're usually not this defensive, but I guess having you yap at them in a language they don't understand is pissing them off. You should probably stay clear of them this time. We'll introduce you in your human form when you change back, and once they get to know you, they'll be okay with this form too. Cats are actually pretty smart. People don't give them enough credit. Now, let's go. We've been invited over to Pete and Willard's house to meet the elders."

It wasn't like I had a choice in the matter, but if I did, I might not have objected to getting out of Damian's house. Maybe these so-called elders could change me back to myself, and then I could report all their asses to the cops.

Damian carried me outside and then put me on the ground, which only served to distract the part of my brain that had been turned into a puppy. I tried to keep up with his long-legged strides by jogging, but then the puppy would see something and off we'd go. I chased a few leaves, my own tail—again—and ran through a mud puddle, before running back to Damian who was all smiles even though I was holding up our forward progress.

Eventually, he did pick me up again. "I know it's pretty awesome to be a pup, but we're going to be late if you keep running off," he said. He petted me while he carried me, and I liked it but loathed it at the same time. Why did it have to feel so good?

Chapter Six

DAMIAN

Willard and Pete's house was all lit up as I approached it with Clay in my arms. He'd been dozing until he heard the howls ringing through the air. Now he was wide awake and trembling slightly, so I held him closer to my chest, trying to reassure him. It had been sixteen years since my first transformation, but I'll never forget the way it felt to be a pup. There were always so many distractions. Having a puppy brain was like having the worst case of ADHD and OCD combined, because once something caught our attention, the thought repeated over and over in our head until we acted on it. It took most shifters a couple of years to get that under control, and there were still times when I found myself chasing a random animal because my brain insisted on it.

"It's okay, pup, you're safe with me. I won't let anything happen to you." I petted his fluffy little head, and he licked my hand. He was damn cute and way less sassy in his beast form. I took the porch steps two at a time, and the door opened before I got to it.

"Oh, look at that. What an adorable little guy," Tracey said. She held out her arms for Clay but I was leery of handing him over. "Aw, come on, you know I love the pups, and mine are all grown now. Let me give him a little sugar."

I reluctantly handed him over because she was an elder and I knew she wouldn't hurt Clay. He squirmed but settled into her arms when she held him close. "He's cute, right?" I asked. I don't know why, but I almost felt like a proud parent as she cooed over him.

"He is. I bet he's a handsome one in his human form too. That's the way it works, you know. Ugly in one form, ugly in the other; that's what my momma used to say." She turned and went into the house, still clutching the pup to her chest.

I followed along behind, the nerves hitting me now that I had to explain myself to the elders. I knew Pete and Willard would have filled them in to some degree, but that didn't mean I wouldn't have a lot of questions to answer anyway. Hell, I wouldn't be in the clear until Clay could transform and corroborate my story.

"Hey there, Damian. I see the transformation was successful. That first one is always a tense time when it comes to the infected. I've seen some that have gone bad, and even a few who died during it," Willard said.

My mouth dropped open upon hearing that. Why hadn't they told me Clay could have died?

"It was better for you to go into it blind." Pete stepped up beside his mate to add. "If we'd have told you all the horror stories, you might have tried to intervene in the process, which would have been bad for the pack. More than once, packs have had problems when someone's called 911 because they thought things were going badly and it turned out everything was fine."

Willard clapped me on the shoulder. "Everyone's first time is different, and some have a tougher time than others. The harder they fight, the more difficult the transition is. You have those who aren't willing to accept the other's takeover, and when they don't relinquish control, the situation ends badly. You seem to have done a great job with this one, though. He seems happy enough."

I looked over to where Tracy had put Clay on the floor among the other younger pups in attendance. Clay was playing with another pup and looked totally at home there.

"Some pups are timid and scared; some will lie there and cry; but yours? Look at him. He's right at home there." Pete's grin was huge as he watched the only not-wolf pup mix it up with the others.

"Yeah, he seems okay, for now. I'm sure once he can talk again, he'll give me an earful. I have to say, though, I like him much better as a pup."

"You don't have much choice in the matter now. You're stuck with that man until he can navigate on his own or until someone else takes him off your hands," Willard said. He led me to the small bar in the corner and poured me a shot of whiskey. "For luck and courage." He raised his glass, and I matched it with mine so we could touch them together before we threw the shots back.

"Okay, people, let's get this thing done so we can get to doing what we all would rather be doing tonight!" Pete announced to everyone in the room.

Everyone found a seat while I stayed standing. There were eight elders who'd shown up for this little meeting, and I was at the center of their attention.

"Well, it looks like we have a new membership that needs considering here tonight," Willard said.

"I think we need to deal with that one first." Old Ted pointed an arthritic finger in my direction.

"We already told you what he told us. There's going to be nothing to deal with if his story bears out." Pete glared across the room at Ted, who flipped him off, and then they both bared their teeth and growled until Tracey broke in.

"Damian has never broken pack law before. He's always paid his dues on time, and he keeps his property in tip-top shape, unlike some of you," Tracey said, sending a look at Ted and earning her own middle finger.

"Let's hear the story from him. I know Pete and Will told us, but I believe in having a firsthand account of the situation before I make a judgment." Colin was a lawyer, and he was the one who kept the pack's legal shit in order. He also kept a book of pack laws that he knew from front to back, so I knew he was mentally making a case against me and eyewitness testimony was something he lived for.

"I agree. Let's hear him out first before we go making any rash decisions," Clarice said. She put her arm around Tracey's shoulder and kissed her cheek as she settled in to hear the tale of my one-night stand that ended with a new pup.

"I met Clay at the Blue Moon." I started, not waiting for any more bickering because I was prepared to defend myself. "We went for a drive down Highway 9 and parked off in that little spot behind that old bait shop. We got in the camper and fucked. He bit me, but I didn't notice it. He told me he swallowed some of my blood. That's the whole story."

"You left out lots of details," Colin said. Eileen, his wife, snickered but kept her opinion to herself.

"Yeah! We want the nitty-gritty details!" Tracey said. She and Clarice giggled when I looked horrified at the prospect of having to tell them the intimate details.

"He doesn't have to give us the details," Willard said, shaking his head at the two older women.

"I want to know how exactly you let a human bite you hard enough to draw blood and you didn't notice it." Ted narrowed his eyes at me.

"It was in the heat of passion, which I'm sure isn't something you can relate to." Minnie, who was the quiet one of the bunch, finally spoke up to get in a dig on Old Ted and chuckles out of everyone else.

"I was out of my mind with pleasure?" I asked jokingly.

"You watch it, sonny." Ted waggled his finger at me, which I wouldn't have even given much notice to but Clay started yapping before he ran over to stand in front of Ted and then seriously started barking at the haggard old man. Ted leaned down and got right in the puppy's face. "And you mind your own business, you little runt." Ted made the mistake of wagging that finger in Clay's face, which only got it nipped. "Oh, you little shit." Ted stood up, but Clay didn't back down.

"Teddy, don't you dare harm that pup!" Clarice hollered before Tracey stood up and grabbed Clay, who kept giving Ted the what-for with all his might.

"You should be ashamed of yourself. Threatening a pup like that," Tracey said.

"He bit me!" Ted looked outraged.

"Yeah, and now you see how it is," I said, not bothering to hide my smirk.

"He's only a pup. You know how they are," Pete said, while he tried to hide his own grin.

"I think..." Colin said but then paused, as if he hadn't finished thinking before he decided to voice his thoughts. "I think we have to postpone any judgment until we can get Clay's side of the story, but your initial thoughts on the subject are right, Willard. If indeed it was Clay who bit Damian, I can't see how we can punish him for that. Clay contracted lycanthropy through his own actions and not through any malicious intent from Damian."

I sighed in relief. "Thank you, Colin."

"Don't thank me. It's the law of the pack, and if we don't live by the law, what are we?"

"Animals." Clarice nodded along with Tracey's pronouncement. "All who agree that we postpone official judgment until we can hear from the other party involved, say yea."

Everyone said yea, even Old Ted, and I couldn't help smiling. It felt like a ten-ton weight had lifted off my chest. Everyone got up, and most of them shook my hand before heading out.

"I'm on pup duty tonight. Would you like me to keep yours for you?" Minnie asked when it was her turn to shake my hand.

"I'd like to take him out for a little while," I said, before looking to Willard and Pete. "Could I use the pen for a bit?"

"Sure, that's a great idea. He should get used to your beast, and a little one-on-one time would be good for the both of you." Pete grabbed Willard's hand and pulled him toward the door, eager to get on with their night of prowling, no doubt. It seemed no matter how old the person got, the nights of the full moon were always something we looked forward to.

"You go ahead and change out in the pen, and I'll bring the pup to you," Minnie said.

I nodded and went out the back door. There was an acre of land that Willard and Pete had enclosed for pup training because wolves were extremely protective of their little ones, and keeping them safe was a big job out in the woods. The pen made it easier to keep an eye on them and also to keep danger away while they learned the skills they'd need to survive as a wolf. Every new wolf shifter's first form was a pup, and from there they grew like a normal wolf through the years. In the first year, new wolves couldn't control their shift and stayed in their beast form for the full three days of the full-moon phase, which lasted around seventy-two hours, give or take a few minutes.

Stripping off my clothes, I stood in the moonlight for a moment, preparing to shift. It was always weird to go from cognitive human thinking to that of the wolf. Though there was a flow to the beast's thoughts, they were less ordered and more primal, focusing on needs rather than wants, and they were very self-centered. Though I would remember everything I did in my wolf form, it was hard to explain the experience to someone who'd never had it. Movies and books never got it exactly right. We weren't wild animals like a real wolf, but we weren't fully aware like a human either; the actual experience fell somewhere in the middle.

"I see you're almost ready for us," Minnie said as she came through the door. Clay followed, nipping at her long, flowing skirt when it moved, but he stopped and stared when he caught sight of me. He cocked his head, and if I hadn't known better, I'd have sworn he was grinning at me. "Your little one had an accident in the house. You'll need to do some potty training later."

The pup looked up at Minnie, gave one sharp bark, then turned back to me. He whined when he saw the stairs, but then he carefully picked his way down to the lawn before running to my side. I bent down and scratched his chin. "Did you make a mess on Pete's rug? He's going to be mad at you." He started yipping at me in response. I knew he didn't understand the human words, but it struck me as funny that it seemed like he did, and in typical Clay fashion, he was mouthing off.

"He's a feisty one, had all the other pups following him around after two minutes. I think you might have snagged you an alpha." Minnie's bright smile covered up for the fact that she had to be kidding. There had never been a case of one of the infected being an honest-to-god alpha, and thinking of Clay made the possibility even more unlikely. Humans couldn't be alphas; even our fearless leader, Pete, was only an omega.

"Funny, Min-Min, really funny."

She shrugged. "Well, whatever, get on with it. I have to get back to the pups before they decide to tear the place apart."

It took only a minute to change. Since I was born into it, and had been taught from an early age to embrace it, there was no pain involved. I howled at the full moon in greeting before turning to look at Minnie. She waved and left me and the pup to do doggy things.

AFTER A FEW hours of playing in the pen with me, I sent Clay back to the nursery with Minnie so I could join the other adults on the hunt. Then, as the sun was peeking above the horizon, I went in to gather my pup to take him home. I dug my phone out of my pocket and took a picture of Clay, who was sprawled out underneath a mound of pups. The puppy pile was one of the cutest things ever, and Clay seemed to be enjoying it as he slept. He didn't seem to mind when I picked him up, snuggling into the crook of my arm for the walk back home. I set him down outside the door to my house and tried to get him to do his duty, but he whined and pawed at my leg.

"If you piss on my carpet, the cats will eat you for breakfast," I said as I opened the door to let him inside. I didn't take a shower, thinking it would help Clay get used to the scent of my wolf if he slept next to me with it still clinging heavily to my skin. I stripped naked before lifting him up and putting him on the bed. With the blackout curtains on my window, it was pitch-black in the room when I lay down.

Clay curled up next to my side and fell back to sleep, his tiny puppy snores bringing a short-lived smile to my lips. I was going to have a hard time falling asleep. Clay seemed to be adapting well, but he really didn't have a choice in his current form. What worried me was what was going to happen when he changed back. I had a lot of explaining to do. If Clay's behavior during my previous attempts at trying to talk to him was any indication of how things would go, I was looking at a very rough road ahead.

Chapter Seven

CLAY

It had been the strangest three days of my life—that's all I could say about that. Damian was a doting and sometimes strange... I have no clue what to call him. If I was indeed a dog, I'd have called him an owner, but that didn't seem right since I was a person and not a dog, and no one can own a person, but he acted like the owner of a new puppy. He made cutesy noises and talked to me like I was a baby. If I had to guess, I'd have said he didn't think I understood a word that came out of his mouth the entire time. He also talked a lot, both to me and to the cats. And oh, those cats! They were on my shit list—that was for sure.

Trying to come to terms with the fact that, apparently, werewolves were real, I knew I wouldn't have believed it if Damian hadn't changed into one in front of my own eyes. I had been thinking up excuses for my own strange situation that had me running around on all fours. Everything from stress, to him drugging my food, to an ancient gypsy curse on my family to explain why I was in the shape I was in. But watching Damian go from the perfectly sculpted, tattooed man glowing in the light of the moon to a full-sized wolf had opened my eyes. Sure, it could have still been my mind playing tricks on me to keep me from going insane after being kidnapped, but at some point, I had to accept that I was not that imaginative and this shit was real.

I hoped I'd change back. Prayed to a god I no longer believed in that I wasn't destined to remain a dog for the rest of my days, so I could change back and kill Damian for fucking me up like this. When my human brain was in control, which wasn't all that often, I plotted my revenge. When the puppy was in control, more often than not, I went with the flow and had to admit it was sort of freeing. But no, I was going to get my pound of flesh out of Damian for what he'd done...as soon as I caught that stupid tail!

It was suppertime on Monday, and Damian once again filled the little bowl with food from the can, but I was sick of eating the same thing and had my eye on his pizza. I'd found that Damian couldn't resist cuteness at all, so I used that to my advantage every time I could. This time was no different. With my nose, I pushed the bowl over to his feet and then cocked my head while staring at the piece of pizza he was holding in his hand.

"No way, pup. This will give you the shits," Damian said. "You're better off sticking to your own food." He nudged the bowl with his toe.

"Oh no way, asshole. I'm having some of that pizza whether you give it to me or not." Well, that's what I tried to say, but it came out as a series of dog noises. I jumped up into his lap. He laughed as he tried to push me off, but goddamn it, I wanted that pizza! Licking his face—yes, it seemed gross, but for some reason it wasn't—usually put him in a good mood, so I wriggled into position. Standing on my hind legs on his thighs, paws on his shoulders, I stuck out my tongue and left a trail of slobber from his stubbled jaw to his eyebrow, making him chuckle as he wiped at it.

I was preparing to do it again when a strange feeling hit me. The world spun, and the niggling feeling was there in the back of my head. Some part of me must have known what was going on because this time I embraced the feeling, and a few seconds later, I—the human me—was sitting there, naked, in Damian's lap.

I pulled my tongue back in and scrambled to get away from the man who'd kidnapped me and had somehow turned me into a dog for three days. The look on his face was as stunned as I felt by the sudden change in my form. I scuttled across the couch until I was as far away from him as I could get when he reached out for me.

"Don't touch me!" I may have gotten a little hysterical at that point.

"Clay, you gotta calm down and listen to me. There's lo—"

"Fuck you, I don't have to listen to a damn word you say! You kidnapped me!"

"I did it for your own good. I swear if I could have do—"

"If you could have what? Could have turned me into a dog without kidnapping me and tying me to a bed? And what the fuck was that! How is that...how are you even possible?" I resisted the urge to cry. I really wanted to break down. I was so thankful I was human again, but there was no way I was going to let Damian see me bawl like a baby.

"If you'd just let me explain, I'll tell you everything."

"And why should I give you the chance to explain anything? Why shouldn't I call the cops and have you explain it to them?"

Damian's eyes widened at the mention of the cops. "You can't do that."

"And why not? Give me one good reason I shouldn't."

"Because you'd be ruining a lot of lives if you did."

"One person is not a lot of lives, Damian."

He grabbed his hair with both hands and pulled at it before resting his elbows on his knees and holding his head. "I don't care about me. I care about the people who took me in when I had nowhere else to go. If you go to the cops about this, they're the ones who will end up paying for my mistake."

"I wouldn't call kidnapping a mistake." I folded my arms across my chest, which only served to draw my attention to my nudity, so I crossed my legs too.

Damian looked up at me, and his strange eyes burned with anger. "My mistake was picking you up in the first place."

Well, that hurt a little, but not as much as it pissed me off. "Fuck you!" I spat as I got off the couch and stomped down the hall to his bedroom. There had to be something in there I could put on so I could leave. I wasn't going to stay there and listen to him when I could be filing a police report. He followed me, which I should have figured he'd do.

"Clay, please, listen to me. I know you hate me and I know that the way I had to do this only made it worse, but please, if you go to the police, one of two things are going to happen. They'll either think you're nuts or they'll believe you and they'll take me in and eventually our secret will be exposed. It might take a while but it will be found out, and where does that leave you? You do realize you're now a part of this, right?" Damian talked while I pulled out drawers and searched for clothing.

I found a pair of track pants and a T-shirt and started pulling them on, but he grabbed the shirt before I could yank it over my head.

"Did you hear me?"

I jerked the shirt, but he didn't let go of it. "I heard you, but I don't care. You can't get away with kidnapping someone and then doing...whatever it is you did to me."

"I didn't do anything to you. You did it to yourself, you fucking idiot," Damian growled at me before letting go of the shirt we'd been playing tug of war with, so I fell back on the bed.

"Oh, that's rich. I did it to myself, huh?" I stood and got chest to chest with him, forgetting about the shirt and my quest to get dressed.

"I don't recall being the one who did the biting." He raised his eyebrows like he'd scored a point, but I was still confused and I'm sure that showed on my face. "Yeah, you bit me, asshole, which means you're the one responsible for turning yourself into a dog. How do you like them apples?" He grinned at me when what he was saying finally sunk in and my mouth dropped open in surprise.

"I...uh...I..." I couldn't think of anything to say to that.

"So maybe now, you can sit down, have a slice of that pizza you were so adamant about having just a bit ago, and we can talk. Or I should say, I can talk and you can shut your mouth for once and listen." Damian didn't wait for my answer; instead, he turned around and left me standing there, speechless.

Turning around, I picked up the shirt from the bed and put it on before walking slowly out into the living room. Damian was on the couch eating a piece of pizza. There were two beers sitting on the table, and I sat down, once again as far away from him as possible, before picking one of them up and guzzling it down. I had a feeling I might need something stronger to get me through the upcoming conversation, but the beer was a good start.

"I'm going back on what I said." Damian handed me a slice of pizza on a paper towel. "I'm going to let you talk but only to ask questions if you need to."

"Fine, but how will I know if you're telling me the truth?" I took the pizza, folded it in half, and shoved most of it in my mouth. "I mean, how can I trust you after all this?" A chunk of food fell from my mouth when I asked the last question, and I picked it off the borrowed sweatpants and popped it in my mouth.

"And you say I eat like a pig." Damian looked mildly disgusted by my actions, but I shrugged. I'd been eating canned dog food for the past three days. I was starving for something different. "What do you want to know first?" he asked before handing me another slice and grabbing one for himself.

"Everything," I said, making sure to swallow the food in my mouth first.

"Okay, but this is going to take a while."

And it did. He started with that night when I'd bitten him and explained the low chances of me actually being infected. The reason behind him stalking me and then finally having to resort to kidnapping me. He told me about werewolves and how they have always been around but, no, vampires weren't real. Then he started talking about the pack, and that's when I started asking questions.

"So, you need me to tell your elders that I bit you, or they'll throw you out of the pack, and since you already left your family's pack, you'd be a lone wolf and would probably end up going feral at some point. Does that about sum it up?" I asked when he told me I'd have to go before the pack elders and testify for him.

"It does, but there's also the fact that you'll need the pack, too, and I can help you with that." Damian opened his fourth beer and my sixth.

"What do you mean, I'll need the pack?"

"You need someone to teach you and to protect you. For the first year, you're not going to be able to control the shift, and you'll be a puppy. Who's going to take care of you for three days a month?"

"I can take care of myself." I was sure I could do it. I just needed to lock myself in my house, leave out enough food for three days, and I'd be fine.

"Do you remember how it was when the puppy took over?" he asked. I nodded. Boy, did I ever. "Do you really think that puppy could survive three days alone? Do you think that puppy wouldn't maybe do something that could hurt himself? Like eat laundry powder or chew on an electrical cord?"

"Shit."

"Yeah, shit. So, you need the pack and after you've grown out of the puppy stage, you'll still need other shifters. You'll need the community. Believe me. I spent a year out on my own, and it was hell."

"But you said there were conditions. What are they?" I sat back and rubbed my belly. I'd eaten way too much pizza and had too much beer, but it felt good to do something so utterly human after being a dog for three days.

Damian sat back also. He turned to look at me, and something in his expression told me I wasn't going to like what he had to say. "They want you to find a mate within the pack."

"What? Why?"

"It ties you to the pack, and it also, in theory, will keep you from spreading your seed to the outside world."

"So, let me get this straight, I have to find someone who lives here in this trailer park to fall in love with and then mate for life?" That sounded like the stupidest rule ever to me and highly unlikely to work.

"There are more of us than those who live here on the compound, but yes, they want you to find a mate within the pack. To tell you the truth, now that you're a werewolf, there's a huge chance you'll want another shifter to be your mate. I mean, think of trying to keep this a secret from the person you love and live with. Oh, that brings me to another thing that finding a mate within the pack keeps to a minimum," Damian said and then paused to take a drink of his beer.

"What's that then? Don't keep me in suspense." I rolled my eyes at him, trying to be all dramatic about it.

"I was thirsty from all this talking. It keeps us from infecting our human lovers to make them like us. As we've gone over, biting humans to infect them on purpose is forbidden, but the temptation is always there when you're married or in love with one. Most packs have rules similar to this one, but they make exceptions on occasion, like for the mate bond, but it's rare."

"And if I don't accept their rules?"

"You'll forfeit the protection of the pack and will be shunned by all of us." He shrugged like it was no big deal, but I was pretty sure it was.

"Will I go feral?"

Again, he shrugged, but then he grimaced. "I don't know a lot about the infecteds. My old pack didn't accept them, and no one talks much about it even here where there's a few of them. We can ask Willard and Pete about it when we go to the pack meeting tonight. And speaking of the meeting, we should probably head over there so we're not late."

"Tonight? There's a meeting tonight?" I was in no way ready to go meet the pack elders.

"Yeah, we always have the meeting after the full moon, so then everyone is in a better mood." Damian stood and waited for me to do the same.

"But... Oh shit! It's Monday, isn't it?"

"Yeah, why?"

"Fuck! I was supposed to work today. I need my phone. I have to call Betty and tell her—"

Damian grabbed my arms and squeezed hard enough to get my attention. "I called in for you. I told them I was a friend of yours who was looking after you because you were sick, too sick to call in. Betty says to get better soon but not to come in until you are because no one has gotten their flu shot yet."

"You called in sick for me?"

"I did, because like it or not, I'm responsible for you until you find a mate in the pack, and you losing your job isn't going to make things any easier on the situation."

"You're responsible for me?"

"Of course. You're my pup until someone else wants you." Damian managed a forced smile as he let me go and chucked me under the chin.

"After what we've done together, you calling me your pup sounds really wrong. Isn't that like saying you're my dad or something?"

"It could be taken that way, or if put in another context, it could mean I own your ass." That grin I hated so much was on his face again, and the old urge to punch it came back.

"Fuck you. You don't own shit, other than this trailer house, that is. I'm assuming you own this." I held out my arms.

"I also own those two big cats that tried to eat your scrawny ass; remember that," he leaned in to whisper.

"I hate those cats."

"The feeling's mutual, I'm sure. Now let's go, it's time to face the music."

I sighed as he handed me a zip-up hoodie from a small closet by the door before putting on his leather jacket. I followed him out into the fading evening light. I was nervous and still reeling from the newness of it all, but one tiny malignant thought entered my head as I stared at Damian's broad back and remembered he was the reason my life had been turned upside down. I could really fuck up his life if I lied to the elders and told them he bit me. Maybe that would be my revenge if I couldn't go to the cops to get it.

Chapter Eight

DAMIAN

My talk with Clay went better than expected, but I knew it was far from over. He was probably still in shock, and once he had some time to process, there'd be a whole new set of questions. I led him into the center of our little town because that's where the community center was—where the pack meeting was held at the end of the third day of the full moon each month. It wasn't required that we attend. Most of the time I didn't, but since I had business with the pack, I had no choice but to go and take Clay with me.

The building, previously an old barn, had been renovated, and now it had a shiny wood floor and bleachers that collapsed into the walls. It was used for all sorts of functions from the occasional pickup game of basketball to wedding receptions. It was a multipurpose sort of space that all small communities had. Tonight, there was a small stage set up in the front with eight chairs on it for the elders, and for the rest of the attendees, there were folding chairs set up in rows facing it.

Clay was glued to my side when we walked up the concrete path, but he was looking everywhere. "I didn't know this was an actual town," he whispered as we got to the door. I'm sure it was strange to see shops set up in houses, but it made it easier to hide in plain sight when you could take down the Pal's Pizza sign and close the blinds to make it look like a normal house. People hardly ever wandered into the town because it was private property. There were no-trespassing signs posted all over, but when the occasional stray did find their way in, precautions were taken to make it look like a sleepy little trailer park out in the middle of nowhere.

"I told you, it's a town that's not a town, and now you know the reason for that." I opened the door, and the sound of a large group of people chatting over each other flowed out. Clay stiffened beside me. "Don't worry. You've met the elders and quite a few of the others who will be here tonight. You'll be fine. They hardly ever put infecteds to death anymore." It was a joke, but I should have known better because Clay clutched at my arm so hard that if I hadn't been a werewolf, it would have left a bruise. "I'm joking. Calm down and try to smile."

I led him into the room, and as with any group of people who all knew everyone who was supposed to show up, all eyes turned to watch the newcomer walk by. I smiled and nodded at each group, who then resumed their gossip once we'd passed. Usually I didn't pay much attention, but this time I knew what they were all talking about because it was about me. I tried not to glare because that wouldn't earn me or Clay any allies with this crowd.

"They're staring at us," Clay hissed in my ear as we approached where the elders were gathered.

"Of course, they are. How often do you think they get the chance to spread such juicy news about someone they already think is beneath them?" I hadn't meant to tell him that I wasn't exactly the favored son of the Outcast pack, but it did explain the intense scrutiny we were under. Clay didn't have time to respond because we'd reached our destination.

"Hey, there they are," Pete said when he spotted us. He looked at Clay and then did a totally Pete thing and pulled him into a big bear hug. "It's nice to finally meet the little pup who stole so many hearts this weekend." He released a traumatized-looking Clay and stepped back. "I'm Pete, and this is my mate, Willard."

"I know. I met you both." Clay then looked at the other elders and pointed to Minnie. "You're Minnie, Clarice, Tracey, Colin, and Eileen, but Ted's missing and I can't say I'm upset about that."

I stared at him because there was no way he should have been able to name them off like that after only spending a few hours with them in his other form.

"Well, I guess we're going to have to let Damian in on our secret since he now has the pleasure of being the responsible party for an infected," Pete said with a conspiratorial wink at Clay, who looked as lost as me.

"The infected werewolves retain their human capability to understand speech, and their thought process is much different than ours. More human than beast from what I've gathered, unless the beast is being insistent. Of course, that's just going on what Pete has told me about his experiences, but it seems like Clay may have had a similar one since he understood and can remember our names." Willard stepped in to explain it to us before holding out his hand to Clay. "It's nice to meet the human you, Clay."

"Thanks, and it's nice to meet you too." Clay was being pleasant, which sent a red flag up in my head. I wasn't used to him not being a prickly asshole, and his calm demeanor made me wonder what he was thinking. It didn't help that his scent was muddled by all the others in the room, so I couldn't tell if the fear was still as strong as when we'd walked in.

"So, this is what all the fuss is about."

The voice sent a chill through me like when someone runs their fingernails down a chalkboard. I had no choice but to turn around and face the person attached to it. "Blaine." The one word dropped from my mouth like a nuclear bomb, and the space around the two of us cleared like a blast zone.

"Hey there, Damian. Didn't know you were back in town." Blaine's smirk said the opposite of his words, but it was only trained on me for a moment before it transformed into a charming smile aimed at Clay. "I have to say, it's a pleasure to meet you." Blaine crowded Clay, who I expected to shrink away from the bigger man, but instead, he puffed out his chest and stood his ground. "Damian always did have excellent taste in men."

"Go away, Blaine," I snarled when it seemed he wasn't going to back off.

Blaine slowly turned his head to look at me. "Oh, is he yours? I mean, I know you infected him, but have you claimed him as your own? Because if you have, the gossip mill is getting rusty. I'd heard he was going to be introduced to the pack as someone in need of a mate. Why else would I be here?"

"No one is going to claim me," Clay said indignantly, staring up at Blaine before he looked to me. "Especially not him."

The only thing I found more annoying than Blaine's voice was his chuckle, and because of Clay's pronouncement, I was treated to that and, for an added bonus, his full-out belly laugh. "Oh, you got a feisty one here, Damian. Remind me to thank you for bringing him into the fold after I've claimed him." Blaine turned on his heel and strode off into the crowd, who'd watched the little showdown between me and Blaine like it was the most interesting thing they'd ever seen.

"We should get started," Willard said. Giving me a sympathetic look, he turned to climb the two stairs to the stage.

Grabbing Clay's arm, I pulled him to the front row of seats that were reserved for members with pack business. He pulled his arm out of my grip and plopped down. He looked really unhappy, but there was nothing I could do about it. I'd told him the pack law, and he'd have to deal with Blaine and any other interested party's advances until he found a mate.

Willard started the meeting, and I should have figured he'd leave me for last because it meant that everyone would stay for the whole meeting if only to see how it played out. "Now, we have one more issue to deal with, and that's the Outcast pack versus Damian Maccon. Damian, come up here and bring Clay with you."

I stood and so did Clay. He followed behind me, and this time the scent of his fear was easy to disentangle from the others. The people closest to us noticed it, too, and I could feel the excitement in the room. If there was one thing wolves loved, it was potential prey, and Clay was broadcasting his vulnerability to them through his sweat glands.

"Damian Maccon stands accused of infecting a human with the lycanthropy virus. How do you plead?" Willard looked at me, as did Clay, whose eyes widened when he realized I was on trial here. This was real.

"Not guilty."

The crowd mumbled because they didn't know the exact circumstances behind how Clay got the virus. This was part of Pete's plan to get the pack to let me stay, because though it was my fault, it wasn't my doing.

"Clay Anderson, testimony has been given by the defendant indicating that it was not his doing that caused your infection. Can you please relate the events of the night of October the twenty-third to the elders?"

Clay swallowed so hard I could hear it. I reached over and put my hand on his shoulder, trying to provide some comfort, which was a mistake, because he shrugged it off and then glared at me.

"I met Damian at the Blue Moon. We went to his camper and hooked up...had sex."

Clay's glare intensified for a moment as he opened his mouth, and I braced myself because, suddenly, I realized he could lie. He could tell them I bit him, and my life would be over. Did he hate me enough to do that to me? Probably, yes. I gave him a curt nod, indicating *do what you will*, and I closed my eyes to await my fate.

"Things got a little heated, and I bit him."

The crowd gasped in surprise at the turn of events. The chatter was so loud that Pete had to use the dog whistle to get everyone's attention once again.

"You all know the rules, so shush or we'll clear the room for the rest of the proceedings." Quiet descended once again.

"So, you bit him. Then what happened?" Willard coaxed Clay to continue.

"I realized I broke the skin, and I swallowed some of his blood accidentally. I washed my mouth out and tried to make myself puke, but nothing happened." Clay was blushing, but he kept his eyes on the elders, not shying away from what he'd done.

"And how did Damian handle that situation?"

"He seemed pissed but then told me he was clean and I shouldn't worry about it."

"He didn't tell you anything about being a shifter at that point?"

"No, he left, and then he started showing up in different places for days afterward. I guess he was trying to get me to like him or something. Looking back, I think maybe he was trying to find a way to get me here for the full moon and figured he could charm me into it, but…"

"But that didn't work, so he had to resort to bringing you here against your will," Willard said.

Clay nodded. "He did and I'm still a little pissed about that, but I'm beginning to see why he did it."

Willard smiled. "Yes, he had a good reason behind his actions. So, to wrap this part up, would you say it was your own actions that caused your infection and not those of Damian?"

Clay's gaze swung to me. "I guess so, though he could give a guy some warning that his blood is toxic."

The crowd chuckled, but I wasn't in the mood to laugh just then.

"Well, I say we put it to a vote, but the testimony seems to bear out Damian's earlier claim. What say you, the elders of the Outcast pack, on the matter of the exile of Damian Maccon for knowingly infecting a human?" Willard called the vote. "All those in favor?" He looked at the other seven on the stage as did I, and the only one who raised a hand against me was Old Ted. He did so with a smug look on his face, even though he would come down on the losing side in the end. He'd gotten his point across—there was no love lost between the two of us.

"All those opposed?" The other seven hands went up quickly in my favor. "The nays have it. Damian Maccon has been found innocent of willfully infecting a human and will remain a part of the pack."

I sighed as the tension of the moment drained out of my body. I'd been somewhat confident I'd be exonerated, but there was always that small chance things could go wrong. They had before. Turning to Clay, I mouthed *thanks* before leaving him to stand on his own before the elders. This was no longer my trial; now it was his turn to stand before them and ask for their acceptance...or not. I wasn't sure which side he'd come down on when it came to asking for the pack's protection and accepting their rules on taking a mate.

"Clay Anderson, you stand before the elders of the Outcast pack as a lone wolf, packless, and at the mercy of said elders. Do you wish to petition for acceptance into the pack at this time?" Willard sounded so official as he asked that I couldn't see anyone refusing.

"Can I have some time to think about it?" Clay asked, making the crowd gasp—me included—for a second time that night. No one had expected that, but the more I thought about what I knew of Clay, the more his answer shouldn't have surprised me.

Frowning, Willard turned to the others on the stage, and they conferred for a few minutes.

I got up and went to Clay. "What the fuck are you doing?" I hissed at him. I'd explained why he needed the pack. Why was he waiting to ask for admittance?

"I need some time to process all this before I make a major life decision, okay? I'm not the kind of guy who jumps into shit without considering his options." Clay didn't look like he was regretting his answer, so who was I to nag him?

"Fine, do it your way," I said, with a shrug, before sitting back down.

"We've decided to give you until the next full-moon phase to decide. You will be provided with the set of rules you'd be expected to follow so your decision will be a well-informed one. I'd also like to extend Pete's offer to counsel you, as he is in the best position to do so. Is this arrangement acceptable to you?" Willard was presenting a blank face, but I was sure he was just as confused by Clay's decision as everyone else in the room.

"I accept the terms. And thank you for extending me this chance. I know it's probably not normal, but it's a huge decision and not one I take lightly." Clay held out his hand, and Willard took it.

"I have a lot of respect for you. You're handling this all with more decorum than I've seen from people born into this."

"Thanks. That means a lot to me," Clay said.

"Damian will be your contact within the pack. If you have any questions or if you come to a decision, he'll be there for you, only a phone call away. I'll get you that packet before you leave the compound."

"Thanks." Clay turned around and looked at me. "Guess I'm still stuck with you for a bit." He walked past me and out the door.

Getting up to follow as Willard called the meeting to an end, I was stopped halfway to the door when Blaine stepped into my path.

"Looks like the feisty one might need some convincing. You need any help in that area, you know where to find me," he said before turning around and joining his gang of asshole buddies.

I rolled my eyes at his back. Like he'd be the one I'd ask for help, and as if he could convince that stubborn ass, Clay, to do anything. I tried to make my way to the door but was stopped by the few people who didn't hate me, with handshakes and congratulations on my win. By the time I made it outside, Clay was halfway down the block, so I had to jog to catch up to him.

"Can I go home now?" he asked without looking at me when I matched my stride to his.

"I'll drive you after Willard drops off that packet."

"Good, I can't wait to get out of this place." He picked up the pace, but then his steps stuttered. "I don't have to move out here if I join the pack, do I?"

"No, I told you there's plenty of pack members who don't live here, but it will depend on your mate, I guess."

"My mate, yeah, can't let me forget about that, can you?" His anger at the situation came through loud and clear.

"I'm sorry, but like I said, it's not as if it's all my fault. You bear some of the responsibility for this mess." I hated that he was blaming me for everything when I'd only wanted to get off.

"I know, and that's what pisses me off the most. I can't just blame you, and that sucks, because if I could, I'd know where to direct all this anger I have. Not like I can kick my own ass, now, can I?"

I reached out to touch his shoulder, but he jerked away. "I'm sorry. I know it's hard, but even if Willard wouldn't have told me I had to be there for you, I'd have done anything to help you until you figure stuff out."

Stopping, Clay turned to face me. "Stop trying to be nice. I'm not a pup anymore. You don't have to act as if you like me. I remember what you said: you hate me as much as I hate you. I won't call you until I've made my decision, and I expect you to stay out of my life until I do."

I stood there like a statue as he walked away from me. I'd have to remember he could understand me in his other form. I had no idea what all I'd said to him while he was a pup and I thought he couldn't understand me. But one thing was clear: I didn't hate Clay as much as I thought I did, because the idea of him out in the world without the pack's protection made my stomach ache.

Chapter Nine

CLAY

Taking advantage of the excuse Damian had made for me, I took two more days off from work. I'd felt fine when he'd dropped me at my front door with the advice to put bars on my basement windows, but then sometime around three in the morning, it hit me; I was no longer a normal human being. I was a freak who turned into a puppy when the moon was full, and that was some fucked-up shit. I crawled out of bed and threw up until I was dry heaving. Then I sat in the shower, still in my sleep pants and T-shirt, until the water ran cold, and even then, I sat there shivering and sobbing until my teeth chattered so hard I was afraid they might shatter.

After dragging my dripping wet ass across the house and into the kitchen, I ate the entire contents of my fridge, then puked it all up. Finally, I grabbed the bottle of vodka from the freezer and changed my clothes. I ended up on the couch with the bottle, the packet of papers Willard had given me, and a Netflix queue full of werewolf movies. I read until the alcohol made the lines too blurry to see, and then I started in on the movies. I passed out halfway through *An American Werewolf in London*, just as the sky was getting lighter.

I WAS BEHIND the counter at work, having taken over for Irene, when I caught scent of the guy who'd just taken a number from the little red box. The hairs on the back of my neck raised, and a growl tried to rise up out of my chest; he was werewolf. He smirked when our eyes met and gave me a little finger wave, but then he went to sit down, minding his own business while I returned to the customer in front of me. Maybe it was a coincidence?

I hit the button, and another customer walked up and gave me their papers. Going through the motions on autopilot, I kept one eye on the other shifter. I fully expected him to come up to my counter when I hit my button ten minutes later, but to my surprise, he went to the one Betty was manning. He didn't even look in my direction again before he left. Maybe I was being paranoid.

Of course, from what Damian said, there were plenty of shifters about, and they needed to transfer titles, renew their registrations, and get driver's licenses like any other upstanding citizen. I wondered how many shifters I'd run into without being aware of their true nature. Even with all those thoughts to reassure myself that it was simply a coincidence the guy had come in to my department, the encounter had still shaken me. "Hey, Betty, could I shut down for a second to use the restroom?" I asked as I tried to steady my trembling hands.

"Sure, are you okay? You look a little pale." Betty motioned for Irene to come and take over for me.

"I'm a little light-headed all of a sudden."

Irene touched my arm and looked up at me with concern, but I couldn't stand there and explain that I was more or less fine. My lunch was trying to come back up, and if I didn't get to the bathroom soon, everyone would be treated to the second coming of my burrito. I made it to the toilet in time, but afterward, I had to stand at the sink and let the tremors run their course. I wondered if this was how it was going to be every time I ran into one of them.

"Do you need to leave early, dear?" Irene asked when I went back out and tried to take my station back from her.

"No, I'm fine, thanks." I wasn't, but I didn't want to make a habit out of missing work for werewolf-related breakdowns. Who knew how many I was likely to have?

"Are you sure you're not having some sort of relapse? You were pretty sick a couple of weeks ago. Maybe it's come back." Betty looked worried, too, but it probably wasn't for my health. It was more likely she was worried I'd spread my sickness.

"I'm fine, and what I had wasn't contagious. I told you that." *Yeah, not unless I bit you or you bit me, for fuck's sake who bites a werewolf?*

I went back to work but I could feel all the ladies I worked with staring at me from time to time and couldn't wait for my shift to end.

OLD HABITS DIE hard, and mine found me sitting in the back booth at the Blue Moon on Friday night, staring at my phone. I'd toyed with deleting my Grindr account, but then where would I find the men I needed to get off with? I knew my last hookup had left my life in the fucked-up state it was in, but then I thought nothing could be as bad as that, right? What was the harm in one quick little fuck? Maybe I could find me one of those straight guys who liked to suck cock. I was on a quest to find one of those, searching the profiles that wanted masc men and went to the extra effort to say no femmes in all caps. Those were the guys most likely to be stepping out on their girls and keeping their love of cocksucking on the down low.

I was about to initiate a chat with one such man when a shadow fell over my table. Looking up from my phone screen, I came eye to eye with the shifter from the DMV. He was leaning over, hands planted on the Formica tabletop.

"Well, fancy meeting you here. Mind if I take a seat?" He didn't wait for my answer, instead sliding into the bench across from me and waving down the waiter. "You weren't waiting for someone, were you?"

"No, I was actually thinking about leaving. You can have the booth." I started to stand up, but his chuckle stopped me.

"It's always the same routine with you, isn't it?" He pulled a cigarette out of a pack, and when he did, I noticed the tattoo on his knuckles—LONE WOLF—one letter per finger stood out on his tan skin in black letters. He lit up, took a long drag, and blew the smoke out at me. "Damn, it's nice to be in these backwater places that still let you smoke when you're having a cold one." He offered the pack to me, but I shook my head. "Suit yourself. You know we can't get cancer, right?"

"I didn't know that, but smoking is a disgusting habit. Kissing a smoker is like licking an ashtray," I said, giving the cigarette that was poised at his lips a pointed look. I wondered how long the guy had been a lone wolf, and if I was dealing with someone on the edge of crazy, since Damian had told me about lone wolves going feral.

"Yeah, well, it's not like you'd go home with me anyway." He shrugged and took another drag.

"What makes you think that?" My brain circled back to the remark about my routine. It made me wonder if I had another stalker on my hands, but this time, one with not so good intentions. I looked at the door, broadcasting my thoughts to the guy sitting across from me.

"I've seen you in here before. You sit here, play with your phone, and drink a few beers. You shoot down any guy who dares get within a couple of feet of you, and then you go home alone. Figured it was my turn to get shot down by the infamous hot guy in the back-corner booth."

The guy got most of the details right. Only I was sure nobody took notice of me sitting back in the darkest corner of the bar and I was not hot. "Well, you're right about you getting shot down; the rest is questionable information," I said, preparing to stand again.

"Nah, it's the truth, but until I saw you the other day in that hellhole where you work, I had no idea you were one of us. Now, why is that?" he asked, tilting his head and studying me with narrowed eyes.

"Maybe your sniffer was on the fritz?"

"Nope, I think it's something else. Something more along the lines of you getting bitten, and now some guy is out there shitting his pants waiting to get thrown out of his pack for infecting a human." The guy grinned like he was proud of himself for figuring out a hard riddle.

"Again, I think you're assuming too much about the situation, and maybe you should mind your own business before you get yourself in trouble." I stood up this time and walked away from the guy. Stopping at the bar to pay my tab, I looked back, and since he was still sitting in the booth, it seemed like I didn't have to worry about him following me.

Stepping out into the well-lit parking lot, I stopped and took a deep breath. My sense of smell was better, and I could pick out all the different aromas of the city, even the dank smell of the lake on the other edge of town reached my nose. It was strange but not unpleasant. I dug my keys out of my pocket as I walked to my car but stopped short when I noticed someone lurking two cars away from mine. It wasn't the creeper wolf from the bar, and as far as I could tell, it was a human. I started walking again, figuring I had nothing to fear from a lone human even if he did seem to be standing there watching me. Just as I was about to put the key in the lock, the guy approached me.

"Hey, you got a light?"

What was it with smokers tonight? Shaking my head, I looked up at the guy who was now only two steps away from me. "No, man, I don't smoke, sorry."

"That's too bad. I really needed something to calm my nerves." He put the cigarette behind his ear and chuckled nervously.

I sniffed because the air around him had changed. I knew Damian could smell fear and probably other hormone-producing emotions, but I was new to this shit, so I had no idea what the scent the guy was emitting meant. I wish I would have realized what it was before he lunged at me, making it clear it was probably adrenaline.

His body hit mine, pinning me against my car. I pushed at his shoulders, and he stumbled backward, giving me room to raise my fist. Instead of hitting him, though, I decided to give him a choice because I was strong before I'd been infected, but I'd noticed I was even stronger now. It wasn't going to be a fair fight.

"If you turn and walk away now, I'll forget this ever happened. Believe me when I say, you don't want to tangle with me."

The guy looked at something over my shoulder before he sucker punched me in the gut. I bent over from the force of it but was able to block the kick he aimed at my head. This time I didn't give him a choice; I punched him in the face. I could feel the bones of his nose break under my fist even before the blood started gushing out. He lay there on the ground, squealing like a stuck pig.

A slow clap coming from behind me drew my attention off the guy I'd hit. I turned around to see Lone Wolf walking in my direction. Fuck, could my night get any worse?

"Nice punch. I wasn't sure you had it in you," he said, stepping around the back of my car and coming to stand over the fallen guy. "You did your job, now get the fuck out of here."

What the fuck did that mean? I looked from Lone Wolf to the guy on the ground, who was trying to scramble to his feet. He grumbled something before running off, still holding his broken nose.

Lone Wolf turned back to me once the guy was out of sight. "I needed to make sure you could hold your own," he said, like that made any damn sense at all.

"What the fuck for?"

"You're a lone wolf like me, and sometimes a lone wolf needs some company. It's not unheard of for a couple or three to team up. Makes it easier to face the world."

"So, you were testing me to see if I was worthy of you?" I snorted and turned to unlock my car. I was done for the night and only wanted to go home and watch a movie.

"What? I'm not good enough for a pretty boy like you?" he snarled before ramming into my back. Once again I found myself pinned to my car, but this time lacking the leverage to shove the guy off. "You think you're too good for me? You think because you hold court in a booth in a dive bar in this pissant town that you're the shit?" he growled into my ear.

I had no idea what he was talking about and had a feeling he might be a bit delusional. Pushing back, I tried to dislodge him, but that only made him press against me hard enough that I could feel his rigid cock against my ass. Fuck, what the hell even?

"Maybe you need to be taught a lesson. Maybe you need to learn that a lone wolf out on his own has to deal with all the other lone wolves on their own. You got no one to back you up, and that's how it's going to be unless you accept a little help. Maybe it will make you see that you need someone like me around." His stinky cigarette breath made the situation all the more real, as he thrust his hips against my ass, telling me just how he intended to teach me his lessons.

"Someone will come out. They'll call the cops and—"

His hand came up to cover my mouth. "Shut the fuck up, bitch."

I was no one's bitch! I bucked my hips and managed to push away from the car a little, but then his hand moved from my mouth to my neck and he squeezed, cutting off my air. I was fucked. He was stronger and was choking me with one hand, even though I was using both of mine to claw at it. I could see the squiggly lines on the edges of my vision that preceded a blackout, but then all of a sudden I could breathe again.

Dropping to my knees when his weight was jerked off me, I gasped for air. Coughing and hacking like I was the smoker, I rubbed my neck, not at all concerned with what had happened to make my attacker stop, until a pair of boots entered my line of sight.

"Hey, are you okay?"

I looked up, half expecting to see Damian, even though the voice wasn't his, but instead, it was the guy from the pack meeting. He held out a hand, and I took it because it would have been bad form to reject help from the guy who saved my life.

"Did he hurt you?"

I touched my neck again but shook my head. "Nah, not really, but he was going to. Thanks for stepping in like that."

Surprise crossed his handsome face as recognition lit up his eyes. "Hey, you're Clay. We met at the meeting the other night. I'm Blaine Whitmore, a friend of Damian's."

"I wouldn't say we met exactly, but, yeah, I remember you." I also remembered Damian's reaction to him, and I was sure calling himself Damian's friend was a stretch.

"I'm not an asshole, really. That was all pack posturing. You'll get used to it. It's what happens when you get a bunch of alpha men in one place, but outside there, I'm the nice guy." He smiled and shrugged as if to say, *oh well, what can you do?* He ran a hand over his tightly cropped brown hair and stood there with his hand on the back of his neck. "Do you want to go back inside and maybe have a drink with me?"

What I wanted was to go home, but how could I refuse a drink with my savior? "Sure. After that, I could use one, but just one. I need to get home and in bed."

"That sounds like it might have possibilities." He winked before putting his hand on the small of my back and turning me toward the bar.

"Don't go getting any ideas. I've had my fill of macho bullshit tonight. It's one drink to thank you for stepping in like that, and then I'm going home alone." I stepped back from him, causing his hand to fall away from me.

"Feisty." He muttered the word but didn't try to touch me again.

My booth in the back was empty, and that's where I headed out of pure habit. I took my usual seat, and he slid in across from me. Blaine was extremely good-looking, but he was one of those guys who knew he was and it made him cocky. He wasn't like Damian who, although he was fucking hot as hell, didn't preen and make it seem like it was the only thing he had going for him. I ordered a vodka on the rocks, and he got a beer.

"So, how do you and Damian know each other, aside from being in the same pack?" I asked. I was thinking this was my opportunity to find out a little more about the man who got me into this shit.

Blaine cocked his head, considering his words before he asked, "Do you two have a thing? It didn't seem like you were together at the meeting. Shit, if anything, I'd say you hated him, but stranger things have happened than two guys who hate each other ending up together."

"We're not together—that's never going to happen." I snorted into my glass before taking a sip.

His smile widened, and it seemed like he relaxed. "Cool. Full disclosure: he and I were together for a couple of years." My mouth dropped open in surprise, but I snapped it shut quickly when he chuckled at me. "I thought that might get a reaction out of you. It's true. I thought he was the one but he broke my heart, and now it's him who can't stand the sight of me. Go figure."

"So what happened?" The question slipped out before I could stop it. I usually didn't pry into people's personal lives, but this was too good an opportunity to give up.

"Sit back and order another drink. This could take a while."

I did just that, and then I listened to the saga of Damian and Blaine, a match made in hell, if his story had even a smidgen of truth to it.

Chapter Ten

DAMIAN

Sitting on my ass, instead of working like I was supposed to be doing, was driving me crazy. I had to call my boss and tell him I wouldn't be able to take that job down in Oklahoma after all, since I needed to be around in case Clay called. That left me with a lot of time on my hands and nothing to do. I got bored. Then I decided to do something stupid, which led me to the Blue Moon, where I got to witness firsthand Clay and Blaine leaving together. They looked damn chummy as they walked to Clay's car, so I didn't stick around to see where that was heading.

My Grindr app got a workout for the next week until I got a call from Pete.

"We need you to come over tonight. We have a situation to deal with." After a curt greeting, Pete got straight to the point.

"Oh, what's it about?"

"I'm sure you've heard the rumors."

I growled because in a small place like this, of course, I'd heard the news. "Clay and Blaine, right?"

"Yep, looks like you're going to be released of your obligation to him sooner than we all thought." Pete sounded as happy as I was about Clay's choice to start seeing Blaine as a potential mate.

"What time do you need me there?"

"We're going to fire up the grill and have a little cookout. It's getting cold and Willard wants to put it in storage soon, so I convinced him to light it up one last time before he does. Maybe around five or so?"

Last thing I wanted to do was socialize with Blaine, but what choice did I have? "I'll be there. Need me to bring anything?"

"Nope, just yourself." Pete paused and then asked, "Are you going to be okay with this?"

I sighed because I'd been thinking that maybe Clay wouldn't be so bad to have around if only I could get him over his anger at being infected. But now he was with the one guy in the pack I had history with. I was sure Blaine was filling his head with a bunch of crap about how much of a dick I was when we were together, making it so Clay would never even think about giving me a shot. I could only sit back and watch as Blaine destroyed Clay like he'd done me because no matter what I said, Clay wouldn't believe me. He thought I hated him. Life sucked.

"Yeah, I'll be fine. It's not like I have much choice in the matter," I finally answered.

"It's not the best-case scenario, that's for sure, but we can only hope that things work out differently this time around, for Clay's sake. See you later." Pete hung up without saying goodbye, but that was his thing so I wasn't offended by it.

I stared at my phone and considered texting Clay. I'd been thinking of doing that a lot lately, but I couldn't get up the nerve. Instead, I played out in the yard with Stumple and Grumpkin who still hadn't forgiven me for the weekend they'd spent locked outside after they tried to eat puppy Clay.

ARRIVING FIRST SUCKED, because it made me look eager, and that was the exact opposite of what I was. I sat in the living room with a beer while Willard and Pete worked around each other in the kitchen. I was amazed at how much it looked like a dance when they moved, each knowing exactly what the other was going to do in time to anticipate their own actions. When Willard had a huge platter of meat seasoned, he motioned to me to get the door, which I did, before following him out onto the deck. It was cold enough that I could see my breath, but my leather jacket would keep me warm.

"I wanted a minute alone with you, so I'm glad you showed up early, for once." Willard checked the flame on the grill and threw a few pieces of chicken on before closing the lid. He put the other meat down on the table and pushed one of the deck chairs with his foot. We sat down, both facing the woods.

"What did you want to talk about?" I asked when it seemed like he needed a push to get him started.

He ran a hand through his long, silver hair before turning to me. "I don't like this situation. I have a bad feeling about it, and I'm afraid your Clay is going to bear the brunt of something he had nothing to do with. He's going to get blindsided by your past with Blaine if you don't tell him about it."

"First, he's not my Clay. Second, he's made his choice, hasn't he? He's coming here tonight to ask to join the pack because he thinks he's found his mate, right? He thinks Blaine's the one already, and I can only imagine how they formed a bond so quickly. Nothing cements a friendship like a common enemy." Willard's silence told me I'd hit the mark on my assessment of the situation. "There's nothing I can tell Clay that he'll believe, and if I'm right, Blaine has already done a good job of making sure I won't even get the chance."

Willard nodded before standing. "You're probably right, but I hate thinking we'll have to put Clay back together when this is all over. Doing it once with you was hard enough."

"Yep, I remember, but I also remember Blaine's trial, and he's still in the pack." Yeah, I was still a little bitter, even two years later.

"You were there for the vote. The only thing is this time the dynamic on the board of elders has changed. If he fucks up again, I'm sure it will be the last time he does so in the Outcast pack."

I shrugged and sat there silently watching him grill enough meat to feed an army while people started showing up and crowding into the house. No one came out on the deck, and I was guessing Pete told them all to leave us alone. I appreciated the extra quiet time before I had to face Clay and Blaine.

"Oh, look at that. You're still the grill master, Willard," Colin said when we carried in the platters of meat. "Are you training an apprentice?" His eyes slid over me like he thought it was a stupid idea to take me on in any respect. Colin didn't like me much, but his fierce adherence to the law kept him from trying to vote me out of the pack, when he knew he didn't have the grounds to do so, unlike Old Ted.

"Damian was kind enough to keep me company out in the cold." Willard was always a diplomat, but he was also one of the few in the pack I considered a true friend.

Everyone descended on the food like a pack of...like they were hungry. I tried to keep my eyes off Clay, but he seemed to be everywhere I looked. Thing was, so was Blaine, and the smug look on his face every time our eyes met had me seething even before anything official had been done to link him with Clay.

After finding a spot in the corner to hide with my plate, I noticed the looks the elders were giving me. I had to wonder if they knew what was about to be announced between Blaine and Clay, why they were allowing it to happen. I was suddenly not hungry and more than a little pissed at all of them for not warning Clay what he was getting into. He wouldn't listen to me, but if one of them pulled him aside, they'd have a chance at getting through to him.

"You're not eating." Blaine had detached himself from Clay's side long enough to come and hover over me to make his astute observation.

"Something spoiled my appetite," I said, raising an eyebrow at him.

"Yeah, I'm sure it must really be eating at you."

"And what do you think is eating at me, oh wise one?"

He bent down to my level so we were eye to eye. "Thinking about that fine ass over there taking my fat cock while its owner begs for more. Too bad you're not enough of a man for him because he's the best little cocksucker I've ever had, present company excluded, of co—"

I was out of my chair before I even knew that I'd planned to pin Blaine to the wall, hands around his throat. "You don't get to talk about me like that, ever," I growled. He grinned, but the pressure I was putting on his windpipe made it impossible for him to respond. But he didn't need to, because as quickly as I'd jumped him, the others in the room had jumped me. I was pulled off him and held back from finishing what I'd started by Willard and Pete at each arm and Colin standing between us for good measure.

"There will be none of that tonight. You"—Pete pointed at Blaine—"remember you're at an official meeting of the elder's council, and you"—he turned to me—"are going to sit back and only speak when spoken to. When your part in this is over, you're going to go home and go about your life like Clay doesn't exist."

I nodded and they released me. When I looked at Clay, I could see the judgment in his eyes. I had just proven everything Blaine had probably told him about me to be true. I slunk off and sat in my corner again, sullenly picking up the plate I'd dropped and waiting for the meeting to officially begin.

I WAITED UNTIL after the next full-moon phase to go back to work. My boss was glad to have me over the holidays, because I didn't mind working on Thanksgiving and Christmas, since I didn't have any family to go home to. I racked up some huge paychecks, but the money did little to assuage the guilty feelings that had started to make it hard to sleep at night. I was the reason Clay was in the situation he was in. Not only him being infected but the shit with Blaine. If he didn't have a vendetta against me, he wouldn't have looked twice at Clay.

I got off work early on New Year's Eve, which happened to be my last day of work on the Oklahoma site, since it was finished. I was supposed to start the drive home, but even the thought of seeing Stumple and Grumpkin again after a few weeks away couldn't get me behind the wheel of my truck. Pulling out my phone, I dialed Matt's number.

"Yeah." Matt, the teenager I paid to take care of my pets, answered.

"Hey, Matt, I know I said I was going to be home in a couple of days, but do you think you could do another week or so? My job is running longer than it was supposed to, and if I leave now, I miss out on the bonus," I lied. He knew how my job worked and usually I threw in a few extra bucks when I got a bonus, so I'd said that to get him to agree.

"Yeah, sure. It's no problem. Since that new guy keeps coming over and taking them out to play, I don't have much to do. You're not thinking about replacing me with him, are you?"

I frowned, even though he couldn't see it. "What new guy?" Who the hell was messing with my cats, and why the hell was this the first I was hearing of it?

"That Clay guy. I mean, I know sometimes I don't do as good of a job as you want, but I promise to do better if you don't fire me."

"I'm not replacing you, Matt. Get a grip. So, how often does Clay come out there?" It made no sense. He hated me, hated the cats, and if he was visiting the compound, it was surely to see Blaine and not to hang out with a couple of felines.

"He's out here, like, three times a week at least. He told me you said it was okay if he played with them. I'm not in trouble, am I?"

I couldn't figure it out, but it wasn't Matt's fault. He could have given me a call to check out Clay's story, but he was just a kid and they didn't usually question adults. "No, it's not a big deal. I guess I remember telling him it was okay to stop by. I was surprised that he was there so often." The lie rolled off my tongue easily. I'd deal with Clay and whatever he was up to when I got home.

"Okay, so it's fine then?" Matt sounded unsure even with my reassurance that he wasn't in any trouble.

"Yeah, totally fine. Give the boys a hug for me, and I'll see you in a week or so," I said, making him laugh at the thought of hugging my two furry beasts.

"Yeah, I don't think so. See you when I see you, bye." Matt hung up after I said my goodbye.

I lay back on my bed and wondered what Clay could be up to with my cats. What possible reason could he have to spend time at my place with them? I gave up when nothing came to mind. Grindr or my hand? I debated a moment before realizing it was the easiest night of the year to pick up a quick fuck at the bar. Who needed Grindr when every single person on the planet would be out, drunk, and looking to hook up?

I DIDN'T HIT any bad weather on my way back to the compound, which was something, considering I drove over the Great Plains in the middle of January, so my drive was uneventful. Pulling into my driveway at just past four on that Saturday afternoon, I was surprised to see Matt sitting on the front porch, bundled up in a parka, scarf, and fingerless gloves, for cripes sake. He was playing on his phone but looked up when he heard my truck. He waved as he stood and pocketed his phone.

"Hey, Matt, you didn't lock yourself out again, did you?" I asked when I hopped down from the cab. I only locked my doors when I was out of town, but at least two of my neighbors had keys, as well as Pete and Willard, since Matt had a knack of locking the door and leaving the key inside on the table next to it.

"Nah, I didn't."

"Then what are you doing out here? It's colder than a witch's tit. The cats aren't being ornery, are they?" Stumple and Grumpkin had been known to guard the door on occasion and attack anyone who tried to get through it. It was a game to them, and sometimes you had to let them get bored before you could get inside.

"Nope, they're out in the backyard with Clay. I was waiting for him to get done so I could put them in and lock up before I go home."

Clay was in my backyard? That was a surprise, not exactly the welcome-home present I was expecting, but at least I'd get my answers as to what he was doing, sooner rather than later. "Why didn't you wait inside?"

"I was but he said he was almost done, so I got ready to go." Matt shrugged like it made sense to him.

"Well, you can go since I'm back and can let the cats in when he's done."

"Thanks, I was sort of freezing my balls off." Matt grinned and turned to walk down the driveway. He was a strange kid, but the only one responsible enough for me to trust with my cats. All the other boys his age on the compound were too busy chasing pussy to bother with making some spending money.

I opened the door and was surprised that I couldn't smell the litter boxes, and this was the first time that happened after being gone for work. It was nice. I was smiling as I kicked off my boots and walked across the living room but stopped short when I caught sight of Clay. He was wearing a snowsuit, lying in the snow, and Stumple and Grumpkin were lying, one on each side of him. All three were looking up at the sky like they were expecting something. I'd never seen my cats lie on their backs like that, and it was weird how still all three figures were, until I tapped a finger on the glass.

Grumpkin was the first to realize his daddy was home, and he stepped on Clay's stomach in his hurry to get to me. Stumple took his time, and Clay, well, he didn't look too happy to be caught in my yard with my cats.

Twenty different thoughts about how I should handle the situation went through my head as I moved back from the door and sat in the middle of the floor to accept my welcome home from my cats. Looking up, I found Clay standing in the doorway, biting his lip as if he was trying not to say what was on his mind.

"Having a good time with these two flea bags?" I asked, trying to start off being civil and hoping to keep it that way.

"Damian, I..." His words trailed off as he stared at me like I was a ghost or something.

"You like my cats." I was trying to tease him a little and he might have blushed, but his cheeks were already red from the cold so it was hard to tell. "It's okay. I'm not mad or anything. I'm just curious as to why you've been spending so much time here with them."

Clay looked guilty. About what I had no clue, but if he'd been on trial, no judge in the world would have believed him if he'd pleaded innocent. "I should go." He turned to step back out on the deck.

"No, wait, Clay. Come in and have a beer, or maybe a cup of hot chocolate to warm up." I wanted him to stay. I wanted some answers, and though I hated to admit it, I'd missed him.

"I shouldn't."

"Why not? Has Blaine already given you the order to stay away from me?"

The look on his face gave me my answer, but then he stepped through the door and pulled his mittens and then his hat off. "Hot chocolate sounds great."

"Cool, I'll go make some." I got up and managed to keep my smile to myself until I'd turned away. Maybe he'd give me a chance to tell him my side of the story, and we could start over. Maybe.

Chapter Eleven

CLAY

I was going to kill that kid, Matt. He had to have known that Damian was coming home, yet there I was lying in the backyard with those monster-sized cats when Damian got there. Fuck my life. After peeling off my snowsuit, I draped it over one of the kitchen stools before sitting on the other one. I didn't know why I agreed to stay. It probably had something to do with the way he'd made it sound like Blaine could forbid me from seeing someone if I wanted to—even Damian—not that I wanted to see him or anything.

"So, how's everything going? How did the last full-moon phase go? Did Blaine start teaching you anything yet?" His barrage of questions threw me because he sounded nervous as he asked them while heating milk and making me the promised cup of hot chocolate. What did he have to be nervous about? I was the one who got caught doing something I shouldn't have and, fuck, if it wasn't embarrassing as hell.

"Uh, the change went well. I don't fight it anymore, so it's not fuck-all painful like the first time."

He snorted as he pushed the mug across to me and then stood with one hip against the counter. "Yeah, that did look painful."

"Ya think?"

"How's Blaine doing as your mentor?" A shadow crossed over his face when he said Blaine's name. It was no wonder why, if what Blaine had told me was true. Damian still had it in for the guy for trying to get him kicked out of the pack after what he'd done to Blaine.

"He's not really been around during the last two times. He..." I let the words die on my lips. Maybe I shouldn't tell him this stuff. It wasn't any of his business anyway since I was no longer his responsibility.

"He what?"

"He needs the nights of the full moon to run with the pack." It wasn't as if he couldn't ask pretty much anyone and get his answers. So what was the big deal if I told him? "I've been spending those nights with Pete and Willard, but mostly Pete since we're the same."

Damian's eyes narrowed. "What about during the day? He takes care of you then, right?"

The blush rose on my cheeks, and I knew my face was red when I picked up the cup and took a sip, trying to hide my expression behind it. "No, I've been staying in the nursery with the other pups. It's no big deal. I actually prefer it." I tacked the last part on when he looked like he was getting ready to murder someone.

"That's bullshit. He's supposed to be the one teaching you how to work with the pack. He's the one who's supposed to take you home in the morning and make sure you're taken care of. I knew this was going to happen." His voice had gone all growly, and I'd been around Blaine enough by now to know that meant Damian's wolf was closer to the surface—that, and the smell of it was much stronger.

"Why do you care so much? It's not like you wanted the responsibility of dealing with me. I remember quite clearly how many times you said you couldn't wait until someone else was the one who had to clean up my shit and feed me." My ears burned at the first one. Man, you shit on a guy's carpet once, and you were all of a sudden too big of a hassle to keep around.

"I was just talking. I didn't know you could understand me. Haven't you ever had a pet? I mean, you talk to them all the time, and most of the time it's just gibberish. It's like having a kid, but you don't have to filter what you say because you know they're not going to grow up and remember all the crazy shit you said in the heat of the moment."

"Which only means you were telling the truth." I shrugged. I was over it. He hated me, and I hated him, so as far as I was concerned we were even. Besides, it's not like I wanted to be tied to some abusive psycho anyway. I'd dodged a bullet when I'd hitched my wagon to Blaine. Blaine was a cocky asshole who I didn't really get along with. I was also seriously getting sick of fending off his sexual advances, but as long as it looked to the pack like I was dating him, it meant I didn't have to look for anyone else.

"You really don't want to hear anything but what you want to hear, do you?" Damian sipped his own hot chocolate, contemplating me over the rim of the mug while he did.

"I don't want to hear lies, and that's pretty much all you've ever told me."

"I don't recall telling you one single lie," Damian countered.

I rolled my eyes and stood. I didn't need this shit. I was going to go out and get laid to release the pressure seeing Damian had added to my already stressful existence on the compound. It had been too long since I'd last used my Grindr app, and my swiping finger was getting itchy.

"See, you're leaving because you know it's true." Damian came around the counter so he was on the same side as me when I reached for my snowsuit. He snatched it out of my hand. "You know damn well that I never lied to you, not once, and now you're pissed because you know I'm right and you're being an ass—"

I grabbed the front of his shirt, swung us around, and pinned him to the glass patio door. "I'm being a what?" My own beast was tickling at the back of my brain like it did when the moon was getting close to full—there, but unreachable.

"An asshole," Damian spat as he pushed at me. It did nothing but piss me off because now I was stronger than him. He was no longer the only one who had the advantage of the wolf behind him.

"Say that again. I dare you." Tightening the grip I had on his shirt, I pressed in closer. "Say it."

Damian's glare was heated when he opened his mouth but then closed it before he said what I'd dared him to say. I leaned in and sniffed his neck, much like he'd done to me on that first night. I could smell fear, which was interesting, but underneath that was something else, something earthy and muskier than the fear. I pushed my body up next to his until we were pressed together from hip to chest, and the meaning of the scent became clear to me through the layers of clothing separating us.

"Say it." My voice was more growl than not when I commanded him to say the words. I wanted him to give me a reason to do something to him. At this point I wasn't sure if I wanted to fuck or fight, and I needed the push of him saying the words again to decide it for me.

He swallowed hard before his bicolored gaze met mine, blinking when a single bead of sweat ran down into his blue eye, but then staring intently at me once more. "You're an asshole."

I tasted blood, but I didn't care. If anything, it excited me even more as I smashed my lips down on his, hard enough to break the delicate skin inside his lower lip. He growled but I growled back and his low guttural sounds turned to whimpers. My inner beast was grinning at my win over Damian. He'd submit to me, and I'd enjoy every second of it.

I ground my pelvis into his, and he returned the gesture with more enthusiasm than someone who was being assaulted should. He brought his hands up. Instead of trying to push me away, he grabbed my shirt, mimicking the hold I'd had on his before. He pushed, making it clear that he wasn't trying to move me away from him, so I let him move me back a step, and he came with me, clutching at my shirt to make sure I didn't get away from him.

Spinning around, I walked us across the room until he ran into the back of the couch. Once I had him somewhat pinned again, I let go of his shirt and ran my hands down his chest to the waistband of his jeans, popping the button before pulling the zipper down. When my hand grazed his rigid cock, still trapped behind his underwear, he gasped into my mouth.

"Tell me you want me to fuck you and I will." I murmured the words against his lips with a confidence I'd never felt when with a man. All signs were telling me he wanted it, but something inside me needed to hear the words. Unlike the first night, I wanted him to ask for it, not command me to do it.

He unclenched his fists from my shirt, and I wondered if I'd made a mistake, but then he twined his arms around my neck. Nibbling at my jaw, he ground his hips against mine, trapping my hand between the swelling bulges in our pants. Retracting my hand, I reached around and grabbed his ass, lifting him to his toes and making him moan against my neck.

"Ask for it. Now, before I change my mind and leave."

Damian stopped moving. I was sure he was going to tell me to go fuck myself, and the thought was only reinforced when his arms dropped from my neck. I took one tiny step back and tried to see what he was thinking, but he kept his head bowed as he turned around. He pushed his jeans and underwear down and bent over the back of the couch, presenting me with his amazing ass. He dug between the couch cushions for a moment before reaching back—a bottle of lube lay in the palm of his hand. I took it and stared at it, not daring to ask why he needed a bottle of lube hidden in his couch because I was afraid the answer was that he did this a lot. The thought made my beast growl, but I didn't know why.

"Fuck me."

I slapped his ass hard. "That sounded like you telling me what to do. Is that what I said I wanted?" I asked before smacking his ass again. I felt so fucking powerful that I didn't even think about what I was doing. The actions came so naturally to me; it didn't even seem strange to be spanking some guy's ass and telling him to ask me to fuck him.

"Will you fuck me?" The words came from his mouth, but he'd clearly struggled to say them.

"What's the magic word?" Okay, I might have been a little drunk with power, and I fully expected him to reject me this time.

"Please?"

I almost dropped the lube when the word came from his lips, but again, my instincts took over, and words came from my mouth without me putting any thought behind them. "Please what?"

Unbuttoning my pants, I then popped the top of the lube, a sound I knew he recognized because his hips moved against the couch in anticipation. I poured the lube on my hand and dropped the bottle on the floor before pulling my cock out. One thing I'd learned from Pete was that the lycanthropy virus killed off every other bug, making it impossible for us to catch anything, and that meant I could fuck Damian raw. The thought excited me to no end. It would be the first time I'd ever fucked without a condom.

Finally I got my answer when he said, "Please, fuck me, Clay. Please."

My knees almost buckled at the pleading note in Damian's voice, but I managed to steady myself as I covered my cock in lube and got into position. Just like the last time, I stopped when the head of my cock breached his tight entrance. I had to hold his hips still so I could enjoy the new sensation of skin on skin when he tried to push back into me. He whined, but I was going to do this my way and he'd have to wait.

"Clay, please, fuck me," he begged, sending me a look over his shoulder that held only need and lust. My beast came closer to the surface than it had ever been when the moon wasn't full. I could feel it lurking there like it was dying to come out. I was exhilarated, but at the same time, a little scared by the feeling.

Snapping my hips, I buried my unfettered erection in the man below me, and that was the end of any real thought for me. The next few minutes were animalistic rutting and grunting until his ass clenched around my cock and he howled as he found his release. My beast responded to the call with its own howl as my thrusts sped up until I spilled my seed inside Damian. I slumped down over him, his sweaty T-shirt pressing against my cheek while I tried to catch my breath.

My beast was pleased by claiming Damian, but I wasn't as happy about it. I didn't know what it meant, and I wasn't going to stick around to find out. Pulling out, I quickly shoved my cock into my pants. Damian stood slowly, and by the time he turned around, I was already grabbing my outdoor gear. I didn't bother putting my snowsuit on all the way, only shoving my arms in the top half while I stuffed my feet into my boots. I avoided looking at Damian while he pulled his pants back up, but my efforts came to a crashing end when he blocked my way to the door.

"So, that's it then?" he asked.

"Yeah, that's it." I tried to sidestep him, not interested in discussing what had happened between us. I'd chalk it up to a hate fuck and try to forget it ever happened, but he moved with me, apparently not ready to let it go.

"You're just going to fuck me and then go running back to Blaine?" He cocked an eyebrow at me, and when I didn't answer, he shook his head. "It's not going to work between you two. I don't know how it's lasted this long. How he hasn't seen it yet, but he will and then you'll be looking for another mate."

"Seen what yet?"

"I'm not the one to tell you. Besides, how could you believe me when all I do is lie to you?" He moved so I had a clear path to the door, but I hesitated.

"If you think being cryptic is going to get me to stay here and talk over what just happened or what's going on between me and Blaine, you have another think coming. I don't give a shit about all this pack crap. I'm only doing what I need to do to survive. Everything else"—I waved my hand to indicate the shit between us and everything else in the world—"is an annoyance I have to deal with until I can handle shit on my own."

I left him standing there, staring at me with his strangely colored eyes. Fuck him and fuck all of this. One day I'd leave it all behind, but until then, I needed to keep up my charade with Blaine.

My car was parked in town in front of the pizzeria. I hadn't wanted people to see it parked at Damian's even though I suspected half the town knew I spent time there with the cats. I'd even lied to Blaine and told him that Matt needed a break because Damian had been gone longer than usual. He'd questioned me about it, but I'd made up the excuse that Matt thought Damian and I were better friends than we were. Seeing the cats was a good excuse to be on the compound for the required amount of time I was supposed to spend there until I found a mate, making it less time I'd have to spend with Blaine.

I had an ulterior motive to parking there: I'd discovered that they made these awesome calzones one day when I was exploring the town, and now I was hooked. Pushing through the doors, I hummed in appreciation of the scents that hit me. I was going to drown out my thoughts about Damian with the extra-large, every-type-of-meat-you-could-imagine, three-cheese, five-pound calzone of death.

I'd have leftovers for the next day, too, which made me grin like an idiot. I couldn't help it. Good food on top of recently having had an amazing orgasm—even one drenched in regret—was making me entirely too happy, that was, until I realized Blaine and his cronies were sitting in one of the booths. Our eyes met and he got up, sauntering across the room like he owned the place. He started to smile, but then his lips turned down instead. I could almost see him scenting the air around him, and I knew I was about to be found out unless I could think quickly.

"Hey, Clay, I figured you'd come in here," he said, stepping in and crowding me. Unlike Damian, who was close to me in height, Blaine was a good six inches taller and built like a brick shithouse, so I didn't much like it when he stood so close that I had to crane my neck to look up at him. He dropped his voice so I could barely hear him. "Want to tell me why me and every other shifter within a mile can smell Damian on you?"

Stepping back, I turned to the counter to put my order in while I tried to think up a plausible excuse, when it hit me. "I was with the cats in his house; of course, I'd smell like him." I shrugged like it was nothing.

His eyes narrowed, and I almost thought I got away with it until he hooked a finger in the front of my jeans and pulled me back to him. I fucking hated being manhandled, but I bit back my growl because it wouldn't be good to start something when his friends were there to back him up. He dug his fingers in until I could feel them in my pubes before he pulled them back out and brought them to his nose.

"Did you feel the need to jerk off while you were there? His scent drive you that crazy?" He didn't hold back his own guttural rumble.

"You're paranoid, you know that? So, I didn't change my shorts this morning, you want to come do my laundry for me so I got clean ones?" I'd intentionally said it loud enough for everyone to hear. His friends snorted but stopped short of full-out laughter when Blaine turned to shoot them an angry glare before training it on me once again.

"Remember what I said about him. You were already pushing it with the cat sitting, but since I'm a sensible guy, I let it go. Don't push me too far on this." He turned on his heel, and his followers got up and crowded around him as he left.

I let out a sigh of relief, but it was short-lived, because when I paid for my order, Pal, owner of Pal's Pizza, leaned over the counter. "I can smell the sex on you, boy. Next time, take a shower before you leave."

I was mortified as I realized the implications of that statement, so I took my carryout box from his hands and fled. Fuck, I was so fucked.

Chapter Twelve

DAMIAN

"Dude, seriously, I don't have all night. My girlfriend gets off work and will be home in an hour. Are we going to do this or not?"

I shook my head and got off the bed. "Nah, man, I ain't feelin' it. I gotta go." Finding my jeans in the mess of dirty clothes on the guy's bedroom floor, I pulled them on while he sat up and lit a cigarette.

"This sucks. I was really looking forward to tapping that fine ass of yours." He loudly blew the smoke out of his nose and stared at me in disappointment.

"Sorry, guess the smell of your girlfriend's pussy on the sheets fucked up my boner." It was a lie, but there was no way I was ready to admit to a Grindr hookup why I couldn't get hard, even though he'd been sucking on my dick like it was a lollipop for the last fifteen minutes. Hell, I wasn't ready to admit to myself why I was having a hard time getting it up with hookups—this was the third failed attempt this week.

"Fuck you, asshole." The guy wasn't pissed off; if anything, he looked pleased that I'd noticed the crusty spots on his sheets.

"I'll show myself out." I pulled on my jacket and made my way through the tiny, dingy apartment to the front door to get my shoes. I didn't even bother tying them because the baby started crying and, fuck that, I was gone.

The cold nipped at my ears as I walked down the street to my truck, frustrated by another aborted attempt to get Clay off my mind. It was time for me to face the truth. I wanted him and only him. I hated thinking of him with Blaine and knowing if I didn't do something about it soon, Blaine would find a way to break Clay, and I'd lose my chance. How had I gone from hating the sight of the guy to waking up with sticky sheets like I was fucking thirteen again after dreaming about him, me, and my couch? Okay, who was I kidding? I hadn't really hated Clay. That was just me trying to chalk my burgeoning feelings up to my attraction being only physical so I didn't have to deal with what a mess I'd made of everything.

I went to the only person I could talk to this stuff about—Willard.

Pete answered the door, and his eyebrow raised when he saw me standing there, uninvited and unannounced, at eleven o'clock on a Tuesday night—the night before the full moon, at that. I knew they'd either be busy getting stuff ready for the full-moon phase or they'd be sleeping to get rested for the days ahead when sleep was in short supply, but I needed help.

"Damian Maccon, to what do we owe the honor of this visit?" Pete asked loud enough to clue Willard in on who had dared to show up on their doorstep.

"Let him in, Pete. We both knew he'd show up eventually but didn't think it would take him this long," Willard said as he walked over to join Pete at the door. "Come on now; you're letting out all the heat." Willard pulled Pete out of the way and into the house so I could step in and shut the door behind me.

After hanging my coat on one of the wooden pegs stuck to the wall, I slid out of my wet boots and followed the guys into the living room. Pete already had the whiskey out, which told me they both knew what sort of talk this was going to be. I plopped onto the couch while they sat in their chairs across the coffee table from me. I downed the first tumbler Pete poured for me and gestured for him to sit back when he moved to pour me another.

"What did you mean you both knew I'd show up here?" I poured my own drink and settled into the fluffy cushions of the overstuffed couch.

They exchanged a look, and Willard must have lost the silent argument because he's the one who answered. "You're here about Clay, right?"

"I guess."

"There's no guessing about it, and you know it, Damian Maccon." Pete's Southern accent came out when he was being sassy. He also used that very Southern way of addressing someone that told you they thought you were an idiot and saying your full name meant you couldn't pretend it was someone else they were speaking about.

"Fine, but it's not like it could work between me and him. I'm not strong enough, and he's human." That right there would be a sticking point with the pack. They'd insist that Clay pick someone like Blaine, who could protect him, because even though I had my suspicions, I knew Clay couldn't be an alpha.

"You may not be a strong alpha, but neither is Blaine." Willard looked to Pete who nodded to confirm his statement.

"But, I thought since he was part of Old Ted's line..."

"Old Ted talks a good game, but he's never been an alpha. He got on the elder's council because he's a gamma, and that's got nothing to do with strength and everything to do with the wisdom that comes with age. Though in Old Ted's case, the wisdom part is questionable." Pete sipped his drink while letting me absorb what he'd told me.

"So, Blaine's not an alpha?" The information shook me because Blaine's beast was strong. If he wasn't an alpha, what was he?

"No, he'll probably end up being a beta to some unlucky alpha couple but never the leader of a pack," Pete said.

"It doesn't matter. Blaine's still stronger than me, and he has Clay, who hates me, by the way."

"You're stronger than you think you are, but we all know you won't come into your true power until the mate bond is fulfilled." Willard raised his hand to stop me when I opened my mouth. "I know you have your reasons for not wanting to consummate the bond, and I'm not advocating for it because it's your choice. As for the situation with Clay, I think maybe you're looking at it all wrong." Willard paused to let me try to think up another angle to view my problem with Clay, but I shrugged when I failed to come up with anything. "Have you ever considered that maybe the reason you're drawn to Clay is because he's an alpha?"

I barked out a laugh that surprised all three of us. "A human, an alpha? How much of this whiskey did you drink before I got here?" They were crazier than me thinking Clay was an alpha. These two knew better.

It wasn't Willard who growled at me and made my beast cower—no—it was Pete. My eyes darted to the other half of the pack leadership. Pete's canine teeth had elongated just enough to tell me who I was dealing with. I put up my hand to ward him off while I looked to Willard who sat there with a smug look on his face.

"Meet the true alpha of the Outcast pack."

My gaze swung back to Pete, who was now back to normal and smiling genteelly at me. "Oh, what big eyes you have, Mister Wolf," he cooed at me.

"And what big teeth you have," I muttered back before downing my second glass of whiskey. "Why doesn't anyone know about this?"

"That's simple. You said it yourself—who would believe a human could be an alpha? You were raised in the community. You know that infecteds are still second-class citizens and no self-respecting genetic werewolf would ever recognize that a human could possibly be above them," Willard said, while Pete nodded along in agreement.

"We've been making a little headway, but the fact that you didn't even consider Clay might be an alpha says a lot about how little progress has actually been made in the area." Pete looked disappointed in me, and to be honest, I was too. I should have trusted my instincts when it came to Clay's power.

"But how do you two hide it?" And the bigger question was: would Clay have to hide what he was too?

"We don't hide it. There are a few who know, but the others assume that I'm the alpha and he's my...Pete."

Pete smiled fondly at his mate. "And you're my Willard."

"Can you guys cool the lovey-dovey stuff? I still have a problem here." I grinned, because it was sort of sweet to see the two old men making goo-goo eyes at each other.

"And just what is your problem, Damian?" Pete asked the question like he didn't know the answer. But of course, if you asked Pete, he knew all the answers.

"How do I get Clay to believe that Blaine isn't the right guy for him?"

"Maybe the better question is, how do you convince him that you are the right one?" Willard asked.

I understood it was a rhetorical question, but I did roll my eyes in response because I got the point. I needed to work on my people skills and maybe accept that being a lone wolf, even if I was part of a pack, wasn't the right way to live my life anymore.

I AWOKE ON the first day of the full-moon phase with the intention of finding Clay before he was forced to change and tell him I wanted a chance to prove I could be the guy he needed. Not only a mate within the pack to make him a part of it, but an actual mate who would be there for him and maybe even love him eventually. It sounded stupid, but I wasn't sure I loved Clay. How could I know if I did when I barely knew the guy? The only thing I knew was that his beast called to mine. That itself surprised me because I'd thought the true mate bond was the only thing that could draw two people together in that way, and I knew this wasn't a true bond since I'd already met my mate—and it wasn't Clay.

Sitting on my couch with my phone in hand, I prepared to text Clay, but a knock on my door stopped me from entering his number. I knew who it was before I opened it. Blaine's scent was as familiar as my own. "You know you're not supposed to come to my house," I said in greeting.

"I think the pack would forgive me this one transgression when they hear what you've been up to." He didn't look happy, and I knew this could only be about one thing—Clay.

"I'm not letting you in, so you'll have to step back and let me get my coat on if you want to talk to me." There was no way I was going to let him into my house and end up alone with him where there would be no witnesses if things got ugly between us.

"Fine, but hurry up. It's fucking freezing out here." Blaine turned around and went down the porch steps to wait in the driveway while I put on my coat and boots to join him.

"Talk fast. I don't like freezing my nuts off," I said when I stood in front of him.

"You need to stay the fuck away from Clay. He's mine." Blaine got straight to the point.

"I would think if he was yours, you wouldn't have anything to worry about." I shrugged, but I was intentionally baiting him into a fight with those words.

"I wouldn't have a problem if you'd keep your dick out of the picture. You're confusing him, and he's only human. You know they're not very bright when it comes to this shit." He stepped up to get into my face, and memories of the bad old days came flooding back. Even though it was cold, I was sweating. He grinned but it wasn't one of those nice sorts of grins, and a chill followed the droplets of sweat down my back. "How cute—you'll fuck what's mine behind my back, but you're still afraid of me."

"You almost killed me. I've got plenty of memories to keep the fear alive and well." I stepped back, trying to create a little space between us so I could draw a full breath, but he came with me.

"You were weak. That was the only reason you couldn't handle me. It had nothing to do with me or how I treated you. It was all you. You were pathetic then, and you're pathetic now." His spittle dotted my face as he told me once again that all the abuse I'd suffered at his hand was my own fault. That I'd deserved every beating, every rough fucking that had left me bloody and torn, and every ugly word he'd ever said about me was true. I was a worthless pile of shit, who didn't deserve to live, let alone have the love of a man like him.

Fear kept me paralyzed. I knew if he started to hit me, I'd stand there and let him until I could no longer remain upright. Then I'd curl up in a ball on the frozen concrete while he kicked me into unconsciousness. I didn't know why I couldn't move when faced with his anger, and it always left me feeling like he'd been right all along. I did deserve everything he'd done.

"Stay away from Clay. If I see you even glancing in his direction, I'll finish what I started."

I could only stand there and stare at his back when he turned and strode down the driveway to his car. Only able to make my feet move when I could no longer hear his engine, I walked back to my house on legs that felt like jelly. I had no doubt he meant what he'd said. He was getting more and more violent as the years went by. It was only a matter of time before he killed someone, and I was at the top of his list.

Once inside, I glanced at my phone, but texting Clay no longer held any appeal. I decided to wait and go over to Willard and Pete's right before the full moon rose to try to catch Clay there. He'd said Blaine didn't go with him, preferring to run with the other alpha-holes instead. Maybe I could convince Pete and Willard to help me make Clay see that Blaine was going to hurt him. Even if he didn't want me, I needed to get him away from Blaine, or his blood would be on my hands as surely as if I had done the deed myself.

WALKING ACROSS THE compound on the night of the full moon meant running into more people than you'd think possible for such a small town. It was because even the pack members who lived elsewhere liked to come out and be among others like them when they shifted. There was a steady stream of traffic heading toward Pete and Willard's. There had been a spike in birth rates in recent years due to the pack offering free child and pup care to anyone who produced offspring and needed the service. I joined the herd heading to the penned-in area outside the double-wide trailer.

"Hey, Damian, what are you doing here?" Matt asked when he saw me. He was standing with his family, which included a chubby infant.

"I came to see if Clay was here yet." No need to hide my intentions since Matt already thought Clay and I were at least friends.

"I think he went around to the back pen with Blaine," Matt said, using his thumb to indicate the smaller enclosed area where parents could work one-on-one with their offspring without the distraction of the other pups.

"Thanks! See you around, Matt." He grinned as I walked off. I wondered why Blaine decided to start taking responsibility, but then it was just like him to do a one-eighty and act the caring boyfriend if it meant he'd get what he wanted. But I started jogging because I had a bad feeling in the pit of my stomach.

I could hear their voices before I got close enough for them to scent me, since I was upwind, so I stopped to eavesdrop before I went any closer. The bad feeling in my gut only got worse when I realized they were arguing and it was over me.

"I told you not to see him, and then when you insisted that you were only doing Matt a favor, I gave in. I let you go to his house, but I sort of figured it was implied that he wouldn't be there when you did. Then I smell his ass on you and you lie to me in front of my friends. Do you know how that makes me look?" Blaine's voice was low and guttural, barely keeping his beast at bay.

"If you're so worried about what your friends think, maybe you should go and try to fuck one of them instead of pawing at me all the time." Clay's voice was almost as deep as Blaine's, telling me he was in much the same state. The only difference was Clay's beast was no match for Blaine's, not this early in his transformation phase.

"Yeah, that's the other thing that pisses me off. You'll let that fucking weak-ass piece of shit fuck you, but you keep denying me every time. You afraid you can't handle a real man?"

I cringed as I waited for Clay to reveal the truth—that he'd been the one who'd fucked me, but that's not where he went. The cringe turned to surprised horror when Blaine's lies came back to bite him in the ass in the form of Clay's accusation.

"He was man enough to fuck you up," Clay spat out. In the silence, I waited for the fight to start. I was tense and poised to get in there to help Clay when it did. Blaine might be able to take either one of us alone, but together I figured we could turn the tables on him. "Remember all those stories you told me about how Damian manipulated you? How he emotionally and verbally abused you until you had no choice but to strike out physically at him? Doesn't sound like such a weak piece of shit to me, now doe—"

The words were drowned out by a familiar howl that sent shivers down my spine. Blaine's anger had gotten the best of him, and he'd shifted. I started throwing off clothes as I ran to the entrance to the pen. I stood there as a horrified Clay stared down a huge gray wolf.

His eyes found me. "Damian, please!" he screamed. I embraced my beast, but not before I watched as Clay disappeared from my line of vision. His frightened yelping reached my ears just as they shifted to furry and pointed. I knocked the gate down and pounced on Blaine right as he lunged at the helpless pup cowering in the corner under a pile of clothes.

I knew I was no match for Blaine in human form, and in wolf form, I was even more unmatched, but I couldn't let him hurt Clay when he was a defenseless pup. Clamping my jaws down on the scruff of Blaine's neck, I held on as he thrashed around, trying to dislodge me. I was hoping if I made enough of a commotion or drew enough blood, it would get the pack's attention and help would come.

I underestimated Blaine's power because it only took him a few seconds to flip me over his back. I landed hard on my side, and he was at my neck before I could recover from the stun of hitting the ground. He lifted me up, his teeth digging painfully through the scruff of my neck fur and squeezing my windpipe. My body went limp as it tried to conserve oxygen. Just as the darkness started to take over my vision, I saw something that couldn't be real. It had to be my imagination because there was no way Clay could have transformed back into his human form. It was wishful thinking on my part that he was standing there stark naked and ready to strike with the shovel he held in both hands over his head.

I welcomed the blackness when it came and drowned out my wishful thinking.

Chapter Thirteen

CLAY

I peed a little—okay, a lot—but the shift had taken me over at the worst time ever. Looking up through the armhole of my shirt at the snarling wolf Blaine had become, I knew I was in deep shit. There was no way I could defend myself against the slobbering beast that seemed dead set on eating me. A flurry of fur and snapping jaws flew into the pen with us, and then Blaine's attention was no longer on me but on the wolf who'd leapt on his back.

I cowered in the corner until Blaine managed to throw Damian to the ground, and the mismatched eyes rolled back into the wolf's head. I realized Damian had transformed and come to my rescue, but it looked like he was going to lose and do so quickly. Blaine had him by the neck when I reached back into my brain and found that faint link to my humanity.

Snow is cold as fuck when you're sitting your naked ass on it. I jumped to my feet—snow is also cold on bare feet— and it was only luck and the full moon reflecting on the snow-covered ground that made it light enough for me to see the shovel leaning against the fence a couple of feet away. I grabbed the handle and took advantage of the fact that Blaine was preoccupied with Damian, so I could creep up on him from behind. I lifted the shovel, fearing it was too late when I saw how limply Damian's body was hanging from Blaine's jaws, but nevertheless, I brought it down on Blaine's back as hard as I could manage.

Maybe I had misjudged how strong werewolves were, or maybe my aim wasn't as good as I thought, because although I did accomplish my objective and Blaine dropped Damian, he turned on me. With Damian's blood dripping from his muzzle, Blaine lunged at me. I raised the shovel and connected with his head. The dull clang of metal against fur-covered bone rang through the air right as the pack entered the pen, witnessing what I'd done.

The wolves didn't attack me. Instead, they sniffed around their two fallen comrades, and then a handful of them shifted back to their two-legged forms. Among those who changed back were Willard and Pete. They hurried to gather Damian into their arms and whisked him away, while three others I didn't know picked up Blaine and followed. No one talked to me, but Old Ted grabbed me by the upper arm and marched me along behind the procession of humans and wolves.

The building that stood beside Willard and Pete's house and that I'd always assumed was a garage turned out to be a fully functioning clinic. I stood there shivering as Tracey, dressed in scrubs, washed her hands before looking over the two injured wolves who'd been laid out on the stainless steel surgical tables. Clarice helped her after she assessed the damage. They left Damian and tended to Blaine, hooking up an IV line and speaking in hushed whispers.

The slight tremors running through my body turned into something more like quakes, and my legs started to give out on me, but before I fell, strong arms wrapped a blanket around me and Pete led me to one of the padded tables that were there for humans. I let him lift me up and set me down on it because I couldn't think to protest his manhandling me.

"Clay's going into shock," he hollered, and then Clarice's face was hovering over mine.

"He forced the change. He shouldn't have been able to do that. He's probably in more serious condition than either of those two." Clarice added a heated blanket to the one Pete had put around me as I tried to think.

"He's powerful for an infected. If this gets out, we might have problems with the council," Minnie whispered.

I hadn't even noticed her in the melee outside, but her presence was comforting since she was the one who ran the nursery. I'd spent a lot of time cuddled in her lap when I was a pup. Not understanding what her words meant but knowing whatever it was couldn't be good, I lay there staring at the elders as they discussed something in heated whispers, throwing the occasional worried glance at me.

My brain wouldn't focus on any one thing for too long, so those thoughts dissipated, only to be replaced by those of Damian. Was he okay? I whimpered at the thought of losing him and, apparently, shock made me not care that everyone could hear me whining like a scared child.

"It's okay, pup." Willard tried to soothe me. Not only with his words, but he also petted my hair and then, getting in close to my face, rubbed his cheek against mine. It worked better than it should have, and then a thought crossed my mind.

"Scratches, scratches behind the ears, scratches." Oh, my god! I realized I'd said that out loud, but it had not come from the human part of my brain. It was then I realized I had puppy brain even though I was in my human form. I'd shifted but not all of me had reverted to human.

Willard grinned down at me as he moved both hands behind my ears and scratched. "You like that, huh?" he asked when I felt the silly smile spread across my lips. God, yes! I loved that. I whimpered and tried to wriggle closer to him, which made him laugh. "I think you're going to be just fine, pup."

"Broken." I pointed at my head to indicate what I was talking about. I could talk, but it seemed my ability to explain myself was impaired, because with my bouncy-ball puppy brain, I couldn't formulate the complex sentence structure I was used to using.

"Why do you think that?" His brows furrowed, and the puppy in me whined because I'd made him unhappy. I really didn't want to be a bad boy, but I was, because I'd upset the human.

"Can't think good."

Willard straightened up and beckoned Tracey over to my bedside. "I think we might have a problem here."

"What is it? Clarice said it was only shock." Tracey looked harried as she ran a hand through her short, curly hair.

"He says he's having trouble thinking and"—Willard lowered his voice, but I could still hear him—"he's exhibiting pup-like qualities."

Tracey looked at me but then turned her attention back to Willard. "I'll have to look some stuff up, but unless you think he's going to die, I need to get back to Blaine and Damian."

"How are they?"

"I think they'll both pull through. Damian's unconscious but seems to be fine. He's already healing his wounds, but Blaine's not healing as quickly as he should be and that worries me." Tracey glanced over at the two wolves. "It's a bad sign. Might mean brain damage or worse."

I whined again. I might have seriously damaged another person, and now he might die. I hadn't intended to kill Blaine. I'd only wanted to save Damian and keep Blaine from coming after me again.

"I think I'm going to take Clay out of here. He doesn't need the stress in his condition. If what I think is true, he won't be able to comprehend what's going on anyway." Tracey nodded as Willard lifted me off the table and cradled me against his chest. It felt weird but oddly right as I lay my head against his chest, the beating of his heart steady and comforting.

I'D SLEPT. WILLARD put me in the nursery with the other pups, who at first had sniffed me and yipped, but then they'd accepted me as one of their own and piled on. I was safe and warm there at the bottom of the furry pile when Pete came in and woke me with a little shake.

"Clay, Damian's awake and he'd like to see you. Do you want to come ou—"

"Yep, yep, yep, gonna go see Damian. Gotta go, gotta go, gotta go now!" And you know what's embarrassing? Licking a guy's face because you can't hide your excitement; oh, and being naked as the day you were born while doing it.

Pete laughed as he wrapped his arms around me to contain my wriggling body. "Okay, pup, let's go see your man." He let me go and got up.

I was disoriented when I stood. My beast wasn't used to standing on two legs, and the perspective from my full height made me drop back to my knees. Fuck! Seriously? I was going to have to crawl around on my hands and knees? A thought hit me and I latched onto Pete's leg out of fear as

I whimpered. What if I was stuck this way? What if I had to live the rest of my life with my beast in control of my thoughts?

"What is it, pup?" Pete asked, getting down to my level to look me in the eyes.

"Change back. Can't, my head. Scared."

"We've got people looking into that." Pete grabbed the sides of my head to focus me when my inner puppy heard a noise it thought it should investigate. "You weren't supposed to be able to shift forms so early. What made you do it?"

"Damian." His name popped out of my mouth without a thought. I guess I wouldn't be able to lie or even skate the truth in this condition.

"That's what I thought. You two aren't fated mates, but you have a bond. You can try to deny that and push him away, because you still hold him responsible for making you one of us, but believe me when I say it's only going to end badly for the both of you."

"Why, why, why, why?" Yeah, okay, fucking puppy was insistent when something grabbed his attention.

Pete only smiled indulgently at me, like he was seeing the small ball of fur I should have been instead of a fully grown, naked man. "Because the two of you are suited to each other. It's why your beasts call to one another, even though Damian shouldn't be able to because he already has—" He snapped his mouth shut.

"What, what, what?"

"It's not my place to tell you his past. That's something you'll have to ask him. I've already said too much." Pete stood up. "Let's go see him now. He's anxious to make sure you're okay. No amount of us assuring him will do what seeing you with his own eyes will."

Maybe it shouldn't have, but hearing Pete say that Damian needed to see me made me happy. My bare butt wagged, which made my puppy turn to look and then it was confused because something was missing. I crawled along the hall behind Pete while my brain repeated one word over and over—*tail*—because I still hadn't caught that dang thing and now it was hiding from me, sneaky bastard.

I'd expected to end up back in the clinic, but instead, Pete led me down the hall and opened a door. There on a double bed in the middle of the room lay Damian. He was propped up against pillows, awake and alert with a white bandage wrapped around his neck, but otherwise, he looked fine as he smiled at me.

I, of course, made a fool of myself by crawling on the bed and into his lap. To make matters worse, my beast decided that sniffing every available inch of Damian on the way there was a good idea. He gave a startled yelp when I buried my nose in his crotch. Lifting my head, I caught the look he gave Pete, before he turned his mismatched eyes to me.

"Clay." My name came out in a husky whisper that had everything to do with the injury the bandage was covering and nothing to do with sex. I whined to indicate my displeasure at him being injured, and he let me snuggle against him.

"Sorry, sorry, sorry, sorry." The word came out of my mouth on repeat even though there were so many other things I wanted to say, like "Thanks for saving my life."

"Stop it. I'm fine and it wasn't your fault." Damian's hushed words only made me feel worse. He was wrong; it was all my fault. If I hadn't been so quick to latch on to Blaine after he'd saved me in the parking lot of the Blue Moon and then tried using him when I thought I saw a way around the pack's stupid mate rule, none of us would be in this situation right now. Yeah, Damian and I would still hate each other, but I'd gladly take that over feeling responsible for almost getting him killed.

"Damian," Pete said, getting both our attention. "Remember, you're supposed to rest your voice. That bite almost completely crushed your vocal cords, and Tracey wants you to give them more time to heal before you talk." Damian nodded. "If you think you can follow those instructions without supervision, I'll leave you two alone, but if not, I'll have to take Clay back to the nursery."

I got up and crawled along the edge of the bed between Damian and Pete. "Nope. Not going. Nope. Staying. Gotta stay. Stay here with mine. Mine, mine, mine." Well, that was awkward, and I'm not sure my thoughts came across in the way I'd intended.

"Yeah, he's yours, but he's also a part of the pack, which makes him mine too. It's my responsibility to make sure he gets better, and if that means taking you out of here, I will," Pete said through the smile on his lips.

I growled because that was the most effective way to get my thoughts about the matter across. Damian put his hand on my back and ran it to my ass, which he patted, before he gave a low whistle. That got my attention better than words would have—seemed words were less effective while I was puppy brain impaired. He patted his lap, and I scampered over to curl up in it—well, I did my best, but in reality, only my head and shoulders ended up on his legs. He beamed up at Pete and gave him a thumbs-up, to which Pete shook his head and turned to leave.

It was weird, lying there in the silence of the room as Damian stroked my hair; so relaxing. I dozed on and off while looking up at Damian's face. I was still worried that my brain would never be normal again, but the human part of me knew, if it remained the way it was, Damian would take care of me. It made the possibility a little less scary.

"WE HEAL FAST. I'm completely fine," Damian said when I pulled at his pant leg to get him to sit down instead of making me supper. I was naked again—yes again—because who knew wearing clothes could be so uncomfortable? It gave me a new appreciation for those poor dogs that had weirdo owners who dressed them up because they thought it was cute. I was also still crawling around on all fours because vertigo was a bitch.

Tracey had given Damian the go-ahead to leave Pete and Willard's on the second morning of the full-moon phase. Even with my fucked-up brain, my human side didn't think two nights in the makeshift hospital was enough, and I just wanted Damian to sit and rest. He had other ideas, though, as he bustled around the kitchen, trying not to step on my hands when I got underfoot.

"Clay, go lay down until it's ready," Damian scolded me for the twentieth time when he tripped over me and almost dropped the pan of meat he was taking out of the oven.

I glared up at him. How dare he treat me like a dog! "Nope. You lay. You lay. Bad Damian."

He chuckled and reached down to scratch under my chin. "You're fucking adorable. You know that?"

I growled and nipped at his fingers before wondering how weird it must be for him to have to treat me like a pup when I was in my human form. I felt bad for being a nuisance and went to lie on the couch until he called me out to eat. My eyes tracked him the entire time as my stomach growled and my brain tried to insist that I should be out there begging for some of that meat. I managed to ignore my beast long enough for Damian to finish making supper.

We were almost done eating when someone knocked on the door. Damian told me to stay while he answered it, but since the kitchen was right there, I was able to see who was standing outside before Damian put his coat on and went out to join the elders on the porch.

Crawling over to the door, I pressed my ear up against it. My hearing was keener since I'd been infected, but they must have walked out into the driveway because all I could hear were muffled voices and an occasional word. I was able to hear Blaine's name, though, because it was repeated so often.

I scuttled away from the door when I heard Damian's footsteps approaching and buried my face in my bowl to make it look like I'd never left, only looking up at him when he'd sat back down. His brow was furrowed, and his lips were turned down in a frown that meant the elders hadn't been there to deliver good news.

"Blaine?" I asked.

Damian licked his lips and scratched his jaw. "He's alive. He's paralyzed—no feeling or use of his legs. There are those in the pack who are trying to build a case against you for banishment." I whined and he tried to comfort me with pets, but it didn't work. Just when I'd decided I wanted to belong to the pack, it looked like I was about to be denied. Damian got up and led me to the couch, patted the cushion next to him, and I climbed up. He wrapped his arms around me and held me.

It was weird fighting the warring emotions in my head. My beast wanted Damian. Hell, my beast pretty much claimed the man, but my human part still loathed what he'd turned me into. Is it possible to hate someone and love them at the same time?

Chapter Fourteen

DAMIAN

Why is it that the only times my phone should be on camera mode happen to be when I'm talking on it?

"Damian? Are you still there? Hello?"

I burst out laughing, which startled not only Pete, who was on the other end of the phone call, but also the three who were on my bed. Stumple and Grumpkin stared at me with twin looks of what I could only assume were extreme displeasure at being interrupted. Clay looked as embarrassed as his pup would let him at being caught trying to contort himself enough to mimic the two cats who had been busily grooming their genitals. Clay was pretty bendy, but no man was that flexible.

"Sorry, Pete, just walked in on Clay and the cats doing something funny," I said. Clay looked relieved that I hadn't said exactly what they'd been doing.

"I can't believe Clay gets along with those animals."

"Well, I don't know what he did when I was gone, but they seem to love him now. Anyway, I'll bring Clay over as soon as I can get some clothes on him. Is that all you wanted?" I wasn't eager to go see the elders, but Pete thought it was best if we were there when Clay should be shifting back at the end of the full-moon phase in case he didn't return to normal. He made a good point that Clay may need more support than I could give, if he were irreversibly stuck being half human, half beast.

"Mostly, but I also thought I'd give you a heads-up about Blaine and his family being here tonight for the meeting. Neither Willard nor I thought it was a good idea, but we were outvoted on this matter. Some of the others wanted to hold a trial at the meeting tonight, but since Clay wasn't able to give testimony in his current state, Colin ruled that pack law mandated, in the case of such an impairment, it should be delayed until next month unless we can come to a settlement before then."

"What sort of settlement?" I was digging through my drawers to find something loose-fitting that Clay wouldn't try to take off the minute I put it on him. I wasn't even sure who was going to be on trial. By all accounts it should only be Blaine, but the members of the pack who had it out for me were pushing for all three of us to stand trial. The elders were split on how to handle the situation since all they had were two contradictory accounts of the events of the night.

"Blaine's family doesn't want you to pursue banishment, because of Blaine's injury, if Clay's story corroborates yours," Pete said with a sigh.

I clicked my tongue against the back of my teeth as I thought about what that meant. Clay crawled over to stand on his knees at my feet, hands on my waist as he looked up at me, cocking his head in question. It was so strange that he could understand and comprehend, but he had no way of articulating his thoughts. I thought of how hard it must be to be a prisoner in his own head. Which was why I said what I did next to Pete.

"It's up to Clay. If he wants Blaine gone, then I'll stand with him on that."

"I completely understand. I'll see you when you get here." Pete hung up, and I put my phone on the dresser.

Plucking out a loose sweatshirt and pants that matched, I looked down at Clay. "Sorry, pup, but I have to get you dressed, or you'll freeze your ass off in the truck on the way to Pete's."

Clay's eyes widened before he dropped down on all fours and crawled over to the bed where he proceeded to try to wedge himself underneath, only succeeding in getting his head and shoulders under before I dragged him out by the ankle. He wriggled and twisted and yelped when I shoved the shirt down over his head. I was lucky his coordination was so fucked up, making his hands almost useless, otherwise, he'd have had the shirt off before I could get the pants on him.

He whined pathetically as he followed me down the hall. There was no way I was getting boots on him, so I threw him over my shoulder and grabbed my keys, depositing him in the back seat of my truck before getting in myself—only to find he'd crawled over the seat.

"You're a bad pup, Clay," I said as I started the engine.

"No, no, no. Damian bad. Clothes bad." Clay growled after his little rant, and I tried not to laugh at him—too hard. He shivered and then looked at me like it was my fault he was cold.

"See, think of how cold you'd be if I hadn't made you wear the bad clothes."

There were a couple of cars parked outside of Willard and Pete's house, but I recognized them and sighed in relief that it was only Tracy and Clarice who'd shown up early. Clay only struggled a little when I picked him up again, and Pete chuckled as he held the door open for us. I put Clay down, and he immediately started in on the clothes again.

"Off, off, off. Gotta get off." He stopped and looked imploringly up at me. I took mercy on him and pulled the shirt over his head. I decided to leave his pants on for the time being, knowing full well he'd get out of them on his own soon enough; it was the shirt that had stymied him.

"I asked Tracey to come early so she could observe him when the time comes for the change to take place. We've been talking over what we might be able to do for him if he stays this way," Pete said as he led me into the living room, Clay trailing behind, because he was trying to get out of the pants.

"Isn't there something written somewhere about what to do about this when it happens?" I asked, not believing Clay could be the only pup who'd ever forced the shift.

"I've talked to my contacts in other packs around the country," Minnie said. She'd gotten down on her knees to greet Clay, who slobbered all over her face in his excitement, preventing her from telling me what she'd learned.

"There's never been a case of an infected forcing the change this early on. Never." Tracey was the one who filled me in.

"So, what does that mean?" I was suddenly more worried that Clay would be stuck the way he was for the rest of his life.

"It means we don't know what to expect in"—Willard looked at his watch—"about fifteen minutes, give or take. It's an unknown because it was a first."

"Yeah, leave it to him to be outside the fucking norm." I looked at Clay, who was playing with Minnie on the floor.

"All we can do is wait and see." Pete clapped me on the shoulder and handed me a glass of whiskey.

I sat down cross-legged on the floor beside Minnie, and Clay forgot the squeaky toy she'd been hiding from him behind her back. He tried to clamber onto my lap but was unsuccessful. I took pity on him and straightened my legs out so he could sit between my thighs. I was suddenly thankful Minnie had distracted him while we'd discussed his possible fate. It would have been heartbreaking to know he understood and was unable to voice his own concerns. I wrapped an arm around his chest and held him close while we all waited for the clock to tick down to the moment of truth.

The silence was almost deafening when Clay's body stiffened against me. He moaned and twisted and then doubled over in pain before screaming in agony. I froze. Then I was being pulled away from him as Tracey and Clarice started doing their jobs, rolling him on his back and checking his eyes and doing shit I didn't think would help ease the pain Clay was obviously in. When life came back to my limbs, I pushed the women away and curled my body around Clay's.

"Don't fight it, please, Clay. Let go and accept it," I crooned into his ear as I ran my hands over all of his exposed bare skin. I had no idea why he'd fight the change when he'd gotten used to accepting it, but I could tell that was exactly what he was doing. I closed my eyes and tried to will him to accept it, not that it would necessarily work, but I was desperate.

It took longer than it should have for him to give up. The reason he'd been fighting so hard became apparent when his body shrank and my hands only found fur. I opened my eyes to find Clay's small pup form, instead of his human one.

There was an audible gasp from those around us. I sat up, and Clay immediately jumped into my lap and started barking at me. I knew he was asking what was happening when he was yipping in my face. I desperately wished I had answers for him, but I knew nothing and neither did anyone else in the room. Clay was an anomaly, and we'd just have to play it by ear and hope for the best.

STANDING ON THE front porch of Clay's house as he danced around my feet, I unlocked the door and opened it. Clay bounded into the house and barked at the door to his room at the top of the stairs. I followed to let him in, not knowing what he wanted, but apparently he didn't either, because he ran around sniffing everything in the room.

It had been Clarice's idea that I should go check on Clay's house after him being gone for almost a week. I hadn't even thought about the fact that Clay had a life he was supposed to be living. I'd broken into his phone and found out he'd taken more of his sick days to cover the full-moon phase, but he was scheduled to work on Monday, which was tomorrow. I'd have to call his boss and see if I could make up a good enough excuse to get him time off without a bunch of questions.

I turned to leave the room, which made Clay bark, but there was nothing that needed doing in there so we were only wasting time. "Let's go make sure you're not going to come home to any nasty surprises in your fridge." I went down the stairs, but he didn't follow me. I chucked all the perishables out of his fridge and tied the garbage bag before setting it by the door to take out to the curb when we left.

I set the thermostat at a lower temperature—no need for him to be paying to heat the house to a comfortable level if he wasn't there. Then I stood there wondering if there was anything else I should do before he finally came down the stairs to sit at my feet and growl at me.

"I'm sorry, Clay, but I don't know what you want." I turned to leave since there apparently was nothing else for me to do, but he wouldn't come. Instead, he hopped up on the couch and barked at me. I shook my head but went over and sat next to him. "You'd probably holler at me for letting a dog on your furniture. You seem like that sort of guy," I said as he laid his head on my leg. Maybe he missed his house? I turned on the television and sat there petting him. Letting him spend some time in his own place was the least I could do.

WE WERE ALL crammed into the small living room of one of the elders of the Aki Pack, who were the local Native American pack. Minnie, who was sitting next to me, had finally struck gold when the matriarch of the Aki pack had agreed to talk to their medicine woman about Clay's situation. Minnie had gotten a call back from the usually secretive pack, and now here we were, ready to hear what their medicine woman knew.

"We're so appreciative of you agreeing to meet with us, Enola," Minnie said as she accepted a cup of tea from the young woman who was serving it. Clay, who was sitting on my lap, and I were the only males in the room since the medicine woman stipulated that was the only way she'd speak with us. So, Minnie, Clarice, and Tracey, instead of Pete and Willard, had come with me and Clay.

"While it is true we prefer to keep to ourselves, I see no reason to withhold our knowledge from others when it's needed," Enola said, her brown eyes looking kindly at the small pup in my lap. "Will you please tell Kimi we're ready for her now?" The woman serving nodded and left through a beaded curtain.

"So, he's been like this since the end of the full-moon phase?" Enola asked, probably to make conversation, since I knew Minnie had already given her the details.

"Yeah, he shifted from this form to human on the first night and then back to this on the last," I said.

"Hum, it is most curious, but Kimi has found at least one account of this happening," Enola said but didn't explain as another young woman emerged from behind the curtain. Enola smiled at her and held out her hand, which the young woman took before sitting beside the matriarch. "This is our medicine woman, Kimi."

My jaw dropped. I'd been expecting an old lady, not someone who looked younger than me.

"Close your mouth, Damian. You're going to catch flies." Minnie elbowed my ribs to remind me of my manners.

"I see Kimi isn't what you expected," Enola said with a grin. I nodded. How could this young woman know anything? "We believe the body is capable of containing more than one soul, and Kimi has been blessed with the soul of one of our great ancestors along with her own and that of her beast. Don't let her appearance fool you; she has knowledge that extends beyond this realm."

I'd have to take her word for it because it wasn't like she could prove it to me. We were only a week away from the next full-moon phase. I wasn't looking forward to another surprise when it came to Clay, so I was willing to listen to pretty much anything anyone had to say about what was going on, even someone as young as Kimi.

The lights were dimmed and a candle was lit as Kimi was handed a cup of tea that gave off a horrible stench. She sipped it and then stared at the candle for a moment before she began speaking. "Years ago, there was told of a man, who like your pup there was an infected. He was believed to be an alpha, though none would recognize him as such within the pack. He was only seven months into his journey with the wolf when he came upon a woman in need of help. Knowing he couldn't provide that help in his bestial form, he shifted and saved the woman's life. She would later become his mate. But his brain was not the same for the next day and a half, and when the last day of the full-moon phase was waning, he shifted to his beast form."

Kimi paused and took another drink of her tea. "This is the only account I have found of this happening, and it was more than seventy years ago. The theory is that since the beast had been denied its time that it forced the human to give it back. The beast is selfish and takes what it wants."

"So, did the guy get stuck in his beast form, like forever?" I asked as I clutched Clay to my chest.

"No." Kimi smiled as she shook her head. "He changed back but only after undergoing a ritual." She put her tea down and leaned forward. "If you want him back in his human form, you must sever that which links him to the beast."

My brows furrowed as I frowned. "What connects him to his beast?"

"His tail, of course." Kimi smiled as Enola nodded.

"I have to cut off his tail?" My voice was a little shrill, but that was nothing compared to the racket Clay started making in my lap.

"It's the only way. On the third day of the full moon, at the exact time he should undergo the change, you must sever his tie to his beast, or he will be stuck in this form forever."

"But why his tail?" It didn't make any sense. Our tie to our beasts was mental, not physical. This was crazy talk. "And are you saying cutting off his tail will cure lycanthropy?"

"The tail is the only thing that doesn't translate into our human forms, which is why it's the physical link to our beasts. And no, it's not a cure; he will still be able to shift. It's only a one-time fix with the ritual."

I looked to the others who'd come with me. They looked horrified but seemed to believe what the crazy woman was saying. I stood, knocking my knee into the table and sloshing tea about but not apologizing for it. "No, there's no way I'm letting you mutilate this pup." I turned and strode out of the house with Clay held protectively to my chest as if they were suggesting we take the knife to him right that minute. He was whining, but I wasn't sure if it was because he'd heard what they'd said needed to be done or if he was upset with me for saying no.

Standing next to Minnie's van, I had time to think before the women came out to join me. Was I doing the right thing by refusing to even think about the ritual? What if it was true and Clay would be stuck if I didn't let them do it? What would Clay want? Would he want to try it even though it might not work? I looked down into his eyes as I asked, "What would you want? What should I do?"

Chapter Fifteen

CLAY

My head hurt. It was like watching a tennis match as they argued over me, and all I could do was watch and bark at them in a language they couldn't understand. Why did dog-speak have to be so random? I'd learned in puppy training with Pete that the barks meant different things, but it was all about the tone and the barks couldn't convey actual thoughts other than "I'm over here" and "Hey, that's mine. Get away." If dogs could communicate with each other, our problem would have been easy to solve because one of them could have shifted. We could have had a little palaver where I would have told them not to touch my fucking tail. And, oh yeah, giving the guy who tried to kill me the choice on whether or not to mutilate me was probably the worst idea anyone had ever come up with, but all I could do was listen. Well, listen and bark.

"That's asinine and you know it," Pete said as he slammed his hand down on the table.

"It's pack law. He was officially bound to Blaine, and Blaine took responsibility for him. You were there. We were all there that night. It means that he's the one who gets to make this decision as if they'd been legally mated," Colin said, pushing his wire-rimmed glasses up his nose before looking down at the papers he'd been reading on and off all evening.

"But in light of recent events, don't you think that we should consider Blaine might not have Clay's best interests in mind when he makes this decision?" Clarice asked, and I barked my approval.

"There's no formal charges against him. So far, all we have is Damian's word against Blaine's. Without Clay's account of the events, I don't see any way we can bring any such charges against him, without filing the same against Damian, which will put us back to square one. One man's word against the other's, which gets us exactly nowhere," Colin said. I growled because the more I listened to his even-toned explanation of why that fucker Blaine was not thrown out on his ear for attacking me, the more I hated the asshole.

"But don't you think maybe we should put some weight on Blaine's prior behavior toward his prospective mate?" Willard asked.

"That was never proven; so, no, it would be inadmissible." I wanted to bite Colin.

"But we all know what he did to Damian. You can't really think it would be a good idea to give him power over someone he feels might harm his standing in the pack. Not to mention someone he knows Damian has a vested interest in. No matter how you try to justify this, it's wrong and you know it," Pete said before standing up and walking away from the table.

I followed him and whined until he picked me up and rubbed my belly. I trusted Pete and Willard and even the women on the elder's council, but it seemed Colin and Old Ted had it in for me. I didn't even know why they did, but it scared me and I wanted Damian. He'd been banished from the proceedings when he'd let his feelings about the council's decision on Blaine being the one responsible for me be known. I'd spend the full-moon phase with Pete and

Willard instead of with him. I wasn't happy about that, but again, I had no way to voice my opinion on the matter.

"Then it's decided. Blaine will have to make the decision on behalf of Clay, and we'll be bound by it," Willard said, sounding as defeated as I was feeling. "I think we should call it a night." Willard dismissed the meeting and the elders filed out of the kitchen.

Pete set me down and I caught sight of my tail. My puppy brain immediately started the familiar chant to get it, but the human part of me was saddened. *I'll really miss my tail*, I thought, as I spun in circles trying to catch the damn thing because it might be my last chance.

I WAS AT the bottom of the puppy pile—my favorite place to sleep when Damian wasn't an option—when voices made my ears prick up. I struggled to get out from underneath all the other fur balls, getting a few annoyed growls in the process, but eventually I was able to walk over to the gate to see Damian whispering to Minnie and gesturing toward the pen I was in. Whatever they'd been discussing left Minnie frowning as Damian made his way over to where I was standing with my front paws on the mesh of the pen.

He knelt so he was face-to-face with me and smiled, but I knew something was off by the way it didn't reach his eyes. "Clay, listen to me and try to concentrate. They're getting ready to start that stupid ritual to cut your tail off to try to force the change. We don't have much time, so I need you to answer one question for me. If you want me to take you out of here and away, even if it means you face the risk of staying stuck in this form forever, bark once. If you want me to leave you here and get your tail cut off, bark twice."

I barked once, then twice and then again because I was so fucking excited! Then I remembered the question and growled. Why did it take him so long to think of this? It was so simple, yet genius!

"Clay, calm down," Damian shushed me as he looked over his shoulder. "If you draw attention, they'll come and I'll be in trouble."

It dawned on me then that the reason I'd been put in the puppy nursery instead of being able to stay with Damian wasn't for my safety; they were keeping me prisoner. They knew Damian wouldn't allow them to cut my tail off, and he'd have taken me away if he'd had the chance. I was pissed, but that was good because it helped to focus my bouncy-ball puppy thoughts to the task at hand.

"Okay, let's try this again, once for I take you away, twice for staying and no tail."

I gave one sharp bark, and he grinned.

"I knew it. I knew you wouldn't want this, but they wouldn't listen to me," he said as he reached over the top of the pen and picked me up by the scruff of my neck. And then I was in his arms, and I knew me and my tail were on the way to safety.

I half expected Minnie to have raised the alarm, but instead, she gave us a little wave as we passed her on the way out. So, I could add her to my list of accomplices—good to know who was on your side at least when it came down to when shit got real. I nearly started barking when Damian turned down the hall and stepped into the bedroom where he'd been convalescing after the attack, but then he went to the window, and I got that we were sneaking out through there.

He dropped down to the ground, with a grunt, but he held on to me so I didn't fall. I could hear the howls all around us. My puppy wanted to respond, but I understood we were still in danger of getting caught. It took all the human control I had to keep the puppy's instincts from giving us away as Damian ran through the woods.

I could see his truck through the trees when it happened. It took only seconds for the wolves to surround us and another couple for one of them to shift and step out of the pack. Old Ted was not a sight to behold when naked, and I hoped for his sake that it was the cold making his cock look like a shriveled old prune.

"Well, well, well, look at what we've got here," Old Ted said as he walked up to Damian. "Do you think we're stupid?"

"I do, but not for the reasons you think," Damian growled. The scent of his wolf grew stronger, and I nearly peed myself in anticipation of it emerging.

"You've fucked up, boy. We knew you'd try something stupid for that mongrel because you're no better than one of those infected pieces of shit. Running away from the mate bond because you're a coward and then trying to get Blaine kicked out of my pack because you're a pussy who can't take a little slap here and there. You make me sick, and I'd happily let you waltz right on out of here with that little piece of garbage if you'd keep right on going, but no, you'll stick around like the—"

Damian threw a punch that knocked Old Ted on his ass. I yipped in celebration, but the feeling was short-lived as the wolves around us growled and Old Ted shifted back into his wolf. I growled back, but it didn't have any effect on them. Looking to Damian, I wondered why he didn't shift so he'd have a fighting chance to at least run away from the pack, but the way he clutched me to him gave me my answer. He was protecting me, even if it meant he'd get injured or die.

Old Ted advanced, but then a howl rang out through the night air. The wolves surrounding us all stood still for a moment before turning tail and bounding off into the woods. When a new set of wolves came up behind us, Damian turned to face them.

"I'm not giving him up," he snarled.

I recognized the wolf in the lead and barked to let Damian know, but I was sure he also knew it was Pete who'd come to our rescue. Pete shifted and held out his hands to Damian. At first, I thought he wanted him to hand me over, but then I realized he was showing his palms as a sign of peace.

"I want you to know I was against all of this, but Ted took it to the pack. With Colin's legal bullshit to back him up, they voted to overrule me, Willard, and the elder's council," Pete said, and finally Damian eased up his grip on me.

"It's wrong to mutilate a pup even if you think it's going to help him. I can't believe anyone would think that was okay and then Blaine? You would let him, of all people, have a say in this after everything?" Damian's voice shook but not with anger; this time it was pure heartbreak I heard coming from him. "I'm leaving the pack. I'm going to ask Clay to come with me, but even if he says no, I'm gone. A pack is supposed to protect every member, even the lowest of them, and you failed to do that. You failed me, and you almost failed Clay."

"Damian, I realize that things have been handled badly but—"

Damian's shrill laughter cut him off. "Handled badly? Is that what you're telling yourself? I respect the hell out of you, Pete, and I love Willard like a second father, but no, *handled badly* is not the right term for the clusterfuck this pack has become."

Pete started talking again, but I wasn't able to focus on his words. It wasn't my puppy brain distracting me this time, and oh, how grateful I was for that. Damian landed on his back with an oomph when I shifted in his arms and my added weight took him off guard, but his arms stayed firmly around my body. I had to struggle a bit to get him to let me go so I could stand up. Several of the other wolves had shifted and were standing around Pete and Willard. I hopped from foot to foot, wondering how they could stand there barefooted in the snow, but then I spotted the man I was looking for and my frozen toes were forgotten.

Punching Colin in the nose was probably one of the most satisfying things I'd ever done in my entire life. Damian hadn't been there to witness that asshole's use of pack law to excuse putting my fate in the hands of that sadistic fuck, Blaine, but I had heard and remembered every word of it.

"What the fuck!" Colin exclaimed as he bent over, holding his gushing nose.

"You aren't fit to give legal advice to a snake," I spat at him, and then I actually did spit at him. I turned to Pete and glared at him too. "You're just as much to blame. I don't care how much I like you—you didn't stand up for me when it counted. You could have let Damian take me away, but you didn't. You let these fuckers decide that I shouldn't have a choice. I'm not an animal, and no matter how it might have looked, I could still think, and you of all people knew that."

"Pack law tied my hands," Pete said, his voice taking on a wheedling quality I didn't like.

"Even knowing that Blaine attacked me, not only in my pup form, but also in my human one? I mean, there's got to be a law against one of those, right?" I asked, but I didn't even care that he'd nodded that, yes, there was a law against one or both. "Fuck pack law. It can suck my dick, and so can all of you fuckers who would have cut off my tail because of some stupid story."

I turned and locked eyes with Damian in the first light of the dawn. "Did you mean what you said?" Damian nodded. "Let's get out of here then. We can go to my place." We didn't look back as we exited the woods and got into Damian's truck, and no one followed.

I was shivering, and he cranked the heat to the highest setting, though that didn't help. He reached behind the seat and pulled a jacket out. I slid my arms into it and zipped up, but still I shook with tremors. Guess it wasn't the cold making me feel like I was going to fall apart.

He made a detour to his house. Opening the door before I could question his decision to hang around the compound when a pack of angry wolves had a bone to pick with us, he hopped out, leaving me to wait. He emerged a minute later with Stumple and Grumpkin. How he managed to wrangle both cats and carry them to the truck at the same time, I'll never know, but I opened the door so he could deposit them on my lap. They sniffed me and then stood, paws on the dash, watching as Damian went back into the house. Maybe they knew something was up because I was watching almost as intently, wishing he'd hurry up and wondering what could be so important that he'd waste time when we should be getting gone.

He carried out cat supplies: litter box, food, and the bed they shared and shoved it all in the back seat before climbing in himself. "I couldn't leave them." His tone was grim, and I wondered if there was a possibility the pack would torch his house or something.

"I don't blame you, and it's fine. I'm just nervous." My teeth chattered loud enough that he gave me a sympathetic look before pulling out onto the road.

I was happy to see my house but not so thrilled with Damian carrying me to the door since I still had no shoes. I managed to keep my grumbling to a minimum when he carried me all the way to the couch, which was a bit of overkill. The cats came to join me just as I thought about going upstairs to get some actual clothes on. It was almost as if they were sent to make sure I stayed put because they made it impossible for me to get up as they each found room for half a body on my lap. They stayed that way until Damian finished unloading their things and set them up in the laundry room off the kitchen. Then they got up and both gave me a look like I'd been keeping them there, before they left to explore.

"I see you're still shivering." Damian stood, looking down at me with his hands on his hips. "Come on." He nodded toward the stairs and then walked away.

Getting up to follow, I was only slightly embarrassed that my bare ass hung out. He'd watched me crawl around naked on all fours for two days, but still it was uncomfortable to be only half-dressed—and the wrong half at that. But I relaxed as the familiar surroundings of my home reminded me of who I was. I found Damian in the master bathroom, running water in the tub.

"I don't think it's the cold that's making me shiver," I said as a violent tremor shook me.

"Nah, I know, but a warm bath is good for more than your temperature." Damian unbuttoned and slid his jeans down and off his legs, before pulling his shirt off, making his intentions clear. I stepped back when he approached me, but he didn't stop and eventually I ran up against a wall. "It will make you feel better. Think of it as a replacement for the puppy pile in the nursery. You know it's all about touch. Let me touch you and make you feel better."

He slowly unzipped the jacket, and I let him push it off my shoulders. "I don't feel like fucking tonight, Damian." The words made him smile but didn't stop him from taking my hand and tugging me to the half-full tub.

He stepped in. "Come on. Or do you need me to lift you in?"

"Don't even try it."

"Get in and I won't."

I stepped over, dunking my big toe in to test the water before committing to it. It was a little warm, but the minute my foot was in, I didn't care. Damian sat, leaning against the back of the tub, and spread his legs, making room for me. I sat and he pulled me flush against his chest, his arms wrapped around my torso. I could feel his heart beating against my back, recognizing the cadence of it from all the times he'd snuggled me in my other form.

"Why did you do it?" I asked once I was settled in.

"Which it?"

"I guess all of them?"

"I couldn't let them hurt you. I'm responsible for you." His hands moved to my stomach, and he squeezed me more tightly to him.

"That's not true. I chose Blaine over you." Saying the words made me want to throw up, but they were true. "I was so stupid. Can you at least forgive me for that?"

"For being stupid? Always." Damian chuckled, and I turned to look over my shoulder at him. "I understand. I can't say what I would have done in your place, so no need to apologize for making the wrong decision when you didn't have all the facts."

"What about leaving the pack?"

"I was considering it anyway. They fucked me over once, and I stayed. This time I couldn't. Unless something changes, I can't go back there."

"You mean, we can't go back there," I said. I raised my hand out of the water and covered one of his with it. I was going to stay with the only person who was looking out for me and not concerned with stupid rules more than my well-being.

"I was hoping you'd say that."

"Don't get too excited. I'm not sure I don't still hate you," I said. His body stiffened behind me, and I regretted the words. "I guess hate is a little strong. Maybe I still sort of dislike you, but that could change."

"I hope you'll see that I'm not such a bad guy... eventually."

I turned my head back around and let it rest against his chest. "I could see that maybe happening." I closed my eyes and let my body relax as he chortled.

Epilogue

DAMIAN

The sound of the door banging shut reached my ears, even though I was upstairs in the bedroom I now shared with Clay. We weren't together-together, but I felt like I was making some headway in the relationship department, and him not making me sleep in the guest room was one of the things I was putting in the win column. I didn't go down to see what had him slamming the door that way because I already knew and was sure he'd be up to tell me as soon as he managed to get past Stumple and Grumpkin. Only moments later, he came stomping up the stairs and into the room where I was packing bags.

"So, they fucking fired me because you couldn't think up a better excuse for me missing a month and a half of work than I was in the hospital in a coma," he said, his eyes darting between me and the duffel bags on the bed.

"Not like I could tell them you were stuck as a wolf pup. Even if I would have taken you in as proof, I'm sure they wouldn't have believed me." I shrugged and turned to throw more of my brand-new underwear in the bag, while his eyes followed my every move. We'd already discussed my excuse for him, and he'd been thankful I'd thought about calling in at all.

"But you had to have known they'd call the hospitals. They're old ladies who I've worked with for years, and they probably wanted to bring me flowers and pies or some shit." Clay didn't sound as angry as I thought he'd be after having lost his job that morning, but sometimes it was hard to tell what would set Clay off. "And why did you convince me to let you call in and ask for more time off? God, why did I let you? I'm an idiot."

"Because how would it have looked if you'd recently gotten out of a coma and were already ready to go back to work? And Betty told me to tell you to take as much time as you needed as long as you were back today because of that other lady's surgery. She sounded okay with it when I talked to her last time. I did the best I could, and I am sorry you lost your job." I was sort of sorry but not. His not being tied to his job meant he'd be more likely to consider the plan I'd made, if he got over being angry with me, that was.

"I guess," he mumbled and finally came all the way into the room, letting the topic drop much quicker than I'd anticipated. "Do you think you're going somewhere?"

"I do." I wasn't going to say more than that—yet.

"And are you going to tell me where, or were you hoping to be packed and out of here before I got back?" He stepped into me, making me take a step back. It wasn't him that made me do it; it was the alpha inside him—the alpha he still didn't know about. His alpha backed me all the way to the wall and then pressed up against me. The part of me that would always defer to the strongest member of the pack only wanted to rub against him, but I kept myself from doing it.

"I was waiting for you but thought I'd get a head start on packing." It was the truth.

"And where are you going?" His words were more growl than not.

"If you'd step back and then give me a second, maybe indulge me just this once…" My words trailed off when he snuffled my neck and groaned.

"Nothing like the smell of fear and arousal." His breath ghosted over my neck as he pulled back. "I know why you're aroused, but what are you afraid of, Damian?"

I swallowed hard, keeping the truth down and away from slipping off my tongue. "It's not exactly fear, just nerves, mostly." He finally stepped back and let me have the room I needed to breathe, to think, and to move. "Will you take a walk with me?"

"It's a little chilly out for a stroll."

"It's not far, only down to the Pub. Please?"

"Fine, if it will make you happy, I guess it won't kill me." He rolled his eyes before turning for the door, but then stopped to ask, "Well, are you coming or not?"

I knew I had a foolish grin on my face, but I couldn't help it. He so rarely gave in to me. In the three weeks we'd been living in his house together, I'd gotten my way exactly twice, and I was going to mark this day on the calendar the same way I did the other two. I grabbed my leather jacket because it wasn't that cold out.

We walked side by side on the gravel beside the highway. I waved to some of the townspeople I'd met, but Clay ignored them, which I'd learned was what he normally did. He knew everyone and they knew him, but he pretended he lived out in the middle of nowhere with no one around. I resisted the urge to grab his hand and hold it as we walked and then berated myself for even having the thought. I was not that guy, and Clay was really not the kind of man who would go around holding hands in public.

We rounded the bend in the road and walked into the parking lot where my truck was parked. "I wondered where your truck was," he said, and I waited to see if he'd say anything else. "What the hell is that? Did you finally decide to move out?" He pointed to the latest model Heartland Wilderness thirty-eight-foot travel trailer that was hooked onto the back of my truck.

"Nice, real nice, Clay." It hurt a little, but I was sure he didn't really mean it the way it sounded.

"Well then, tell me what this is, if not that." Clay turned to me, and I realized he wasn't happy about this development and his comment was a cover-up for how he really felt.

"Well, you remember how I told you about my job and how I travel all the time?"

He nodded but then cocked his head. "So, you have a job and you have to leave...today?"

"*We* have to leave today." I tried to make it sound like he didn't have a choice, but he shook his head and then chuckled. "I got you a job with my company if you want it. It's way better money than you were making. I bought that with cash." I pointed at the forty-thousand-dollar trailer, and his eyes widened.

"You're rich?"

"No, I'm not, but I live cheap most of the year when I'm working and living on the compound was cheap, too, so I saved my money, but that's beside the point."

"Then what is the point?"

"The point is I want you to come with me. My company has a six-month job down in Alabama, and we can both work on it. I bought the trailer so you and me and the cats could be comfortable. What do you think?" I don't think my heart had ever beat so hard before as it did while I waited for his answer.

"So, we'd be living in that thing during tornado season in Alabama?"

"I'm from there. I survived years of it, so I think you can survive one summer."

He didn't look convinced, but then his frown turned into a grin. "I guess I got nothing better to do, and I've never been down South before. So..."

I grabbed him up in a bear hug and gave him a sloppy kiss, before I thought about what kissing Clay in the middle of his small hometown might mean. He gave me five seconds, and then he pushed me away from him and wiped his mouth with his jacket sleeve. "Don't do that again," he growled before looking around to see if anyone had noticed.

"Sorry, you took me by surprise and I'm happy." I tried to shrug off the hurt and reminded myself that he'd said yes and that was more than I'd expected from him.

"It's fine. Just don't do it again out here, where people can see."

We drove the truck back to his house. He went to his room, taking his laptop with him, to get things in order for him to be gone for six months while I loaded everything up. I was carrying Grumpkin to the truck when Clay came out of the house with his laptop bag slung over his shoulder. I put Grumpkin in the cab and went to take his bag. He grinned but didn't say anything about my excitement.

I pulled out onto the highway not long after noon, which meant we'd probably have to pull over for the night unless Clay wanted to take turns driving straight through. That was something we could discuss on the way, so I set the cruise control once we hit the interstate and drove.

"I'm glad you asked me to come," Clay said after a long silence. He reached over to where my hand laid on the seat and covered it with his.

I turned my hand so it was palm facing up and squeezed his, surprised when he didn't pull away right afterward but, instead, let me hold it for a moment longer. "I'm glad you said yes."

Hey, progress was progress, and I'd take anything I could get.

Acknowledgements

As always, a big thank-you to my crew: Tonna Saunders and Jamila Lindsey, thanks for having my back through this crazy trip. And also to BJ Toth for being the best editor a comma-deficient author could have (she'll have to edit this for commas too, I'm sure). Oh and Happy Birthday Ashley Fae!

About the Author

CL Mustafic is a born and bred American Midwesterner who mysteriously ended up living in a tiny Eastern European country. Left with too much time on her hands—let's be honest here, it was the lack of television channels in her native language—and too many voices in her head trying to fill the silence, she decided to give her lifelong dream of writing a novel a shot. So now between shuttling kids back and forth from various activities, risking her life on the insanely narrow, busy streets of her new hometown, she loses herself in her own made-up world where love always wins.

Email: clmustafic@gmail.com

Facebook: www.facebook.com/clmustafic.author

Twitter: @CL_Mustafic

Website: www.clmustafic.com

Other books by this author

Falling for Him
Loving Sarajevo
"Satin Secrets" within *Beneath the Layers Anthology*
Glory Hole to Hell
Christmas Cookies
Trouble's on the Way (Outcasts, Book Two, Aug. 2018)

Also Available from NineStar Press

Connect with NineStar Press

Website: NineStarPress.com

Facebook: NineStarPress

Facebook Reader Group: NineStarNiche

Twitter: @ninestarpress

Tumblr: NineStarPress